AF446248

FABLE OF REDEMPTION RECLAIMED

A Fantasy Anthology

Edited by Allison Filiatreault

GRAB A FREE BOOK!

This one's on us.

Over a 10,000 year history, the people of Soria have seen bloody wars, the rise and fall of empires, and pitched struggles between dragons and unicorns —the very children of the gods who created men. It is from the dusty volumes in the grand depositories of the world's greatest cities that we look back on the history of Soria and the tales of Metal and Magic.

ofmetalandmagicpublishing.wordpress.com/

Join our mailing list and get your first free ebook!

TABLE OF CONTENTS

Fantasy is a timeless genre that has always been more than a means of escape from daily life. Fantasy creates worlds of dreams and metaphors and offers readers a separate way of thinking. It allows us to tackle timeless issues in diverse ways, all while entertaining. It allows writers and readers alike to experience terror, love, suspense, laughter, and tragedy through a wide cast of characters on journeys of growth or discovery. Fantasy tales connect us to the world by letting us experience their trials and tribulations. Every story offers the reader something priceless: an encounter with another world that will stay with them in their imagination. Here we plunge into a variety of original worlds and journeys with many exciting characters new to the fantasy genre. Please enjoy our newest anthology FABLE OF REDEMPTION RECLAIMED.

Allison Filiatreault, Anthology Editor

The Twilight Guide

by Ryan Cutler

It was already dark by the time Kelton was back on the road to Quilum, much later than he had initially intended. Yet again, a quick tavern break had turned into many hours of drinking and shallow distractions.

The courier cursed himself for his bad habits. He was already close to losing his job, and this latest letter was especially important–the magistrate was expecting it by morning. Instead, Kelton's late departure meant he was several hours behind schedule. Riding throughout the night was his only option, even if it was ill-advised for anyone traveling alone.

Kelton pressed his legs against his horse, causing it to snort loudly before moving into a gallop along the country road. There were certainly worse mounts than the stallion he'd been assigned, though he doubted even the fastest horse could make up for time already lost. Nevertheless, Kelton had no choice but try. Failing this time would sunder his reputation for good. He could already imagine the magistrate rising from his bed to find his desk empty of letters, then spreading word of Kelton's negligence back to his family and employers.

Kelton was still stuck in his head, deliberating what he would tell them, when a figure stepped out into the road in front of his mount. Instantly brought back to reality, Kelton pulled on the reins and drew the horse to a slow stop. He started to call out but faltered as a sharp blade in the approaching figure's grip caught his attention. Kelton's eyes widened. He reached for his own short sword until a harsh voice caught him from behind.

"Hands off your weapons. Let's not make this difficult."

Kelton glanced over his shoulder to see a thuggish male moving out of the darkness, blocking off the road. This man wielded a similarly threatening sword. The initial brigand continued forwards, and Kelton could see the man was dressed in ragged clothes. The man also wore an unpleasant grin on his scarred face.

"Just hand over your horse," the brigand said. "Empty your pockets and we'll be on our way. Unless you want to be removed first?"

Swallowing, Kelton considered his options. If he returned home empty-handed, that would be an even worse fate than arriving late to Quilum. But he would not fare much better trying to fight these thieves, who were clearly more experienced combatants.

With the two brigands closing in, Kelton glanced about his surroundings, quickly spotting a dirt-trodden path to his left. He made his decision. With a kick and a sharp tug on the reins, his horse turned to gallop off the road into the nearby forest. Kelton knew he was heading into unknown territory, but there was little else he could do without failing his mission or losing his very life.

A panicked glance over his shoulder revealed the pair, who had initially given chase, were now hesitating. It was as if they were afraid of the forest. This proved fortunate, as the trail all but ended, and Kelton soon found himself driving his horse through thickening underbrush. The gloomy night engulfed the courier and his mount as they rode deep into the treacherous wilderness. But turning back was not an option.

After a short while, Kelton finally allowed his horse to slow, eventually bringing it to a stop. He could no longer hear the shouting of the bandits on the wind nor catch sight of them through the trees. It was only then that Kelton sobered up enough to realize he could no longer see the path, any path. His long ride through the maze of twisted trees made everything look the same. There was nothing to indicate which way to go next.

The moon lingered in the sky, but the thick canopy of overhanging branches ensured only passing glimpses of its presence. Letting out a heavy sigh, Kelton used his fingers to sweep his short, chestnut curls away from his face as he tried to absolve his rising concern. Turning back would mean facing those brigands again. Any other direction would only take him further towards unknown dangers.

Suddenly, there was a flash of light in the trees ahead. Kelton tensed up and watched as it slowly advanced towards him from the undergrowth. Remaining on horseback, he initially eyed the saddlebag holding his short sword, before readying the reins to take off at the next sign of threat. The young man swallowed, wishing he were braver. He braced himself for whatever came next.

It took another few minutes for a hanging lantern to eventually poke out from behind a tree, followed by a man dressed in dark hooded robes. Kelton rubbed the horse's neck to keep it calm, taking a deep breath to steady his own nerves. The stranger shuffled closer.

"Greetings there," the man said, shifting the lantern to reveal a long grey beard and warm eyes beneath his hood. The illumination caught flecks of silver across his black robes, twinkling like small stars. "What brings you to this part of the forest? Are you lost, lad?"

"That is my business. With whom am I speaking?"

The old man lifted a wrinkled hand to pat the horse on the nose and offered a toothy smile up towards the courier.

"I am Halvor, a priest of the Twilight Order. But maybe you should be answering my questions so I can help you on your way, hm? I know a stray traveler when I see one."

Kelton hesitated at the offer of assistance, especially after his previous encounter with strangers. He'd never heard of the Twilight Order before. However, his situation was dire enough for him to give in. He sighed.

"I'm a courier. I hoped to reach Quilum to deliver a letter before morning, but I ended up leaving a lot later than I had planned. Then an encounter forced me to escape through the forest and now... I don't know where I am at all."

"I can certainly see that. You'd be wandering all night trying to find a settlement out here. Let me show you a shortcut back to the main road. It should save you some time."

"Are you sure? Do you know this area well?"

"It is one of my many duties to help wayward travelers lost in the dark. You will not be the first or the last."

Kelton nodded, beginning to dismount before the priest shook his head. Stepping closer, the old man extended a hand for the horse's reins and adjusted his grip on the lantern in the other.

"Stay where you are, lad. I can lead your stead just fine."

Kelton paused at this, then slowly sat back down, handing the reins to Halvor. The old man gave another smile and tugged the horse as he slowly led them in the direction he'd appeared from. The courier remained on edge yet found some comfort from the illumination afforded to them by the swinging lantern. Its golden flame held off the encroaching darkness. His eyes soon caught the silver sparkles upon the black robes again, and Kelton's thoughts returned to the organization the old man had mentioned.

"Might I ask who the Twilight Order are?" Kelton asked, breaking the silence. "And what are you doing out here by yourself?"

"The Twilight Order... Where to begin... I assume you're aware of Ellea and her place in the pantheon?"

"The goddess of night?"

"The very same." Halvor faced him and grinned like a teacher praising a young child. "But long ago, it was recognized that while Lady Ellea shares the status of her counterparts, she is left out of many prayers due to the opposing hours she inhabits. That's why the Twilight Order was formed, so there would always be acolytes to honor her when she is present."

"Why walk the woods so late alone? Don't you have a temple of worship?"

"Near Ardeth, yes," Halvor called back over his shoulder as he led the horse onward. "However, my order believes we are closer to Lady Ellea when we walk the world at night. The darkness brings comfort to us through her embrace, so we try to offer the same to others."

Kelton nodded a little, sounding a quiet hum of acknowledgement. He could still only assume the priest was leading them in the right direction, but there were no other options for the moment.

The distant howl of a wolf came suddenly from the shadows. Kelton flinched. The beast seemed close by, and he couldn't help but scramble for his sword. Perhaps there would be a fight this night after all.

Halvor placed a reassuring hand on Kelton's arm and shook his head. The old man was impeccably calm.

"How can you find comfort out here when there's so much to hide from?" Kelton wondered aloud as he glanced in the direction of the eerie noise.

"Think of it this way," replied Halvor with the same reassuring tone. "In the daylight, you usually know exactly where you're going, how to get there. You know which path to take to avoid danger. It's the same for us at night, because this is how we've lived so many years of our lives. I know which way is safe and which is not. For example,"–Halvor pointed to where the beast was still howling–"I know there's a wide river between this shortcut and the nearby caves, so those wolves can't come this way. Not those wolves, at least."

Kelton did not find the last point reassuring.

Deciding not to question this further, for his own peace of mind, Kelton returned his gaze forwards again. They continued onward. The idle chatter continued sporadically, though it was largely one-sided due to the courier's keen interest in this strange way of life.

Over the course of the journey, Halvor told the story of how he had stumbled across Ellea's temple as a wandering vagrant and was brought into the Twilight Order by the other priests. It was not so long ago. A once well off life had suddenly turned to destitution, and Halvor had blamed the gods rather than his own bad habits. But the priests of Ellea had convinced him there was a purpose to it all. The tragedy had led him to the forest, to the order. Ever since, he had spent his evenings out in the wilderness, to be as close to his goddess as possible. Having the open sky above him was an added benefit that other priesthoods did not share. Whilst Kelton was not a religious man by any means, it was clear how passionate Halvor was about his order.

Eventually, Kelton's wandering gaze noticed the surrounding trees were becoming less clustered. He sat upright in the saddle, squinting through the lamp light until his eyes widened in surprise. They'd made it back to the highway! And he knew immediately where on the road they were. It would only require another hour of riding to reach his destination.

"I see the road to Quilum!" he exclaimed. "I'll be able to make it by morning now! How can I repay you, Halvor?"

Letting go of the reins, the priest gave its nose a few more affectionate strokes, then shook his head. He turned to give Kelton another smile.

"You owe me nothing, lad. It was my pleasure to help a lost soul find their way through the darkness. Lady Ellea will be smiling upon me for having assisted you. That's all we in the Twilight Order wish for."

Kelton started to protest, but the look of sincerity from Halvor caused him to relent. Sighing, he nodded in understanding and reached forward to take the reins.

"Thank you for helping me, it means a great deal. Without that shortcut and your guidance, I would have been..."

He trailed off, unable to find the words to describe the uncertain future he had narrowly avoided.

"Don't mention it, everyone needs a little assistance sometimes. Besides, you can use that route anytime you like now. Just look out for the spruce trees and keep to the left side of the river, as I mentioned. Oh- and give my regards to Magistrate Cartwright once you reach Quilum."

Kelton slowly panned back to look down at Halvor, his mouth hung open in surprise. His bewildered expression caused the priest to start chortling upon receiving the reaction he had wanted.

"Aldrich is another member of the Twilight Order, one who keeps himself very busy in the court of Quilum these days. Why else do you think he would be awake to expect letters in the dead of morning?"

Halvor gave another toothy grin, reaching up to gently rest his hand on Kelton's arm. Stepping off to let the traveler leave, the old priest held his lantern high in farewell.

Regaining his composure, Kelton returned a grateful smile before he rode off to join the highway beyond the trees. He sent a wave over his shoulder, only to see the old man had already turned away to continue his nightly travels.

Kelton had a lot to think about this morning. The fact that an old man like Halvor could change his life around and find a true purpose meant Kelton could fix himself as well. He resolved, on that stretch of morning road, to clean himself up for good. And this shortcut through the forest could be the very thing to lift his stature as a courier. He couldn't help but smile at his rising fate. Did Ellea have a hand in it?

Kelton then returned his focus to the road, feeling less apprehensive about his arrival. He knew he would soon be in the safe hands of the Twilight Order once more.

THE END

The Rover's Tale

by DonnaRae Menard

From his seat atop the bull camel, Zarda could hear the plodding of wide feet, the humming song of the camel whisperers, and then suddenly, above all else, a shrill shriek. A hundred eyes searched the horizon for danger, But Zarda knew where the trouble lay. Daub.

"Hep," said Zarda, urging the camel forward. The beast negotiated the shifting side of the dune with ease until Zarda was directly behind the selfish, childish boy. Toutia shushed her son, watching over his head as Zarda approached, but Daub did not listen. Again, he screamed his displeasure.

"Daub," barked Zarda.

The boy swung about, stepping back into the moving leg of his mother's beast. The kick sent him flying forward, and the boy landed face first on the hot sand.

"Go!" Zarda pointed toward the rear of the caravan.

"Father Zarda," Toutia pleaded, but Zarda ignored her. Her sad eyes followed her wayward boy as he rushed away.

The boy trotted along the line of animals. Riders averted their eyes, hiding both displeasure at his behavior and embarrassment at his plight. Zarda rode behind Daub, the long legs of his camel pushing the boy along. The last of the caravan was a high, two-wheeled cart, followed by two guardsmen. The desert of Garos was not a safe place to be drawing undue attention, and one needed always to be watchful. Zarda was tired of explaining this to the boy. Perhaps after a day laboring in filth, he would remember.

Zarda left Daub at the edge of the caravan, ordering a different boy away. This boy was more than happy to leave the cart used to collect the droppings of the camels, which were used as fuel for the cooking fires. The old driver never dismounted. Whichever boy assigned the dirty task would gather alone. If he failed to collect a single piece, he might collect a whipping instead. There was no waste when you carried all you owned on your back.

In the evening, Zarda found Daub sleeping beside his mother. He could often be found arguing with his mother, and despite being the eldest boy-child of Zarda's second son, he was an arrogant rascal. Though Zarda tried to be patient, the danger the boy's antics posed to the caravan could only be tolerated so much.

Neither parent remarked on Zarda's treatment of the child because it was his responsibility to keep them safe. Daub's screams put everyone in danger. Though there was no water where they stopped, Zarda had brought them to a place where their encampment would be on a hard-pan surface. The foul-tempered camels would be comfortable through the night, but the goats and the humans had much to fear.

While Zarda watched the sleeping boy and considered the next day's trek, a pair of riders entered their camp. Zarda could tell from their dress these men had traveled back from the next oasis.

"Generous Benefactor," said Jampker, a cousin. "We were hopeful to catch you before you traveled this far, but pleased not to have missed you entirely."

"Rest, eat," said Moulle, Zarda's wife.

Zarda served his cousin a cup of rose water, a required hospitality for close relations. Three generations of Jampker's family had resided at the oasis, but that land had eventually fallen to Zarda through his own father. While they ate, Jampker told how Zarda's eldest son had been badly injured in an attack on the smaller caravan he was guiding. There had been several fatalities, and the troupe had detoured north to the desert border, to a place where they could rest and regroup.

Having been awakened by the commotion of Jampker's arrival, Daub sat behind Belon, his father, listening to the news.

"It is bad," said Jampker. "Besides the loss of family, several camels were taken. Much merchandise was stolen. The drovers are unsure if they should turn back." He leaned toward the old man. "What is your wish, Uncle? Craid and I will ride from here to deliver your orders."

Zarda rocked back and forth. If his eldest son was so badly stricken that he could not command his men, then he was surely mortally injured.

"Who attacked?" asked Zarda. "Marauders or wild beasts?"

"Marauders," said Jampker.

Zarda walked to the edge of the circle, gazing north. He remained there for several minutes. No one approached him. When he returned, his heart felt troubled, and his concern was reflected in the faces of his company.

"It is still a distance from here to the oasis," Zarda said, "but perhaps, two days' travel to Jadabba. We will split the caravan. You, Jampker, return to the oasis with the passengers and the silks. When you arrive, wait for three days. If you do not hear from me, then bring the men to me. While you are gone, double the guard, but leave the women behind. They will be safe within the oasis."

This was not what Jampker had expected. The younger man's expression revealed his confusion. Zarda did not casually leave such important business to others than his own sons.

He turned to his drovers. "We will take the rest of the cargo to Jadabba. Prepare to ride north."

"Mother," yelled Daub, running towards her, his voice cutting through the night.

"Quiet!" she snapped, throwing out her hand to strike him down.

Eventually, Zarda rose from his seat to send the children to their beds. Moulle turned away, ordering others to separate the supplies they would need. Toutia stood over Daub, watching Belon and his father make their plans. Zarda was their leader, and held ownership of all the animals, bred to be the largest camels that challenged the dangers of the desert. This was his caravan. There were others, also ferried by animals he owned. He was the master of many. But this one, this Rover band, was his home group.

Knowing the next few days meant traveling through an area where marauders had already attacked his holdings, Zarda considered sending the women and children with Jampker. He expressed his concern to Moulle. While others slept, they held a heated, whispered argument.

"The caravan will be smaller with less protection," he pointed out. "There will be fewer to share with the duties."

"My back is strong," said Moulle.

Zarda knew better than to continue. He rose, returning to the dead fire for a chance to rest his mind and perhaps sleep. To his surprise, the space he coveted was not empty. The wafting odor of pipe smoke led him to another. The second man sat in the darkness, lost in his own thoughts. Zarda laid his hand on the other man's shoulder. They were old friends, and the man could be trusted.

"Tell me," the man said, "of your plan."

"I will go to my son, but I would ask a boon of you," said Zarda.

The man bowed his head. "You are my master. It is through your generosity my family has a safe place to live. Ask."

"My nephew is an untried youth," Zarda eased down to the sand, pulling his pipe from his robe as he did so. "It is time for him, like the falcon, to spread his wings. I cannot be there to guide him. His own father has long gone to his final rest. I ask that you ride on his right side as guide and mentor."

The man bowed his head in acknowledgment. Zarda dug out one last glowing ember to light his pipe and sighed as his concerns for Jampker eased.

At first light, Zarda sat atop a dune watching as the exceptionally large caravan split ranks, one section moving eastward, the other to the north. His dark-colored camel was as its master, watching, heavy-lidded eyes unblinking, as the trail of its fellows moved below. When the final division had been made, man and beast descended, and Zarda brought up his animal to a trot, moving to the head of the northern-bound line.

Daub rode with his father. All the children rode atop, no one was alone. If marauders happened upon them, they would find this party prepared. Zarda ensured everyone kept watch in the event of danger, for among the ever-surging dunes besides marauders there were the side-winding neromafped. Closer to the foothills was the added danger of snarling blue and black pantsers, and soaring griffins.

On the second day, Zarda was riding at the rear of the line, Daub settled in the seat behind him, when a neromafped rose out of the sand on the side of the dune. At a glance, he estimated this one at only a few heads over his own height in length. It's flat, segmented body honey-hued, revealing youth, and hopefully, inexperience. The hungry predator advanced, its front, clawed appendages stretched out to attack. Zarda knew those claws to carry a venom that could drop even the largest man.

The neromafped lunged at a small camel, swiping with its claws. The injured animal jerked to the side in response, disrupting the line, but Zarda was already reacting.

"HEP. HEP," he shouted.

The camels, even those in the front of the caravan, responded immediately. They were well trained and knew Zarda's voice. The pace increased, and their ropes dragged along those behind. Zarda rushed at the neromafped, which wasn't prepared for the much larger kicking camel and the man's spear. Daub wrapped his arms tightly around his grandfather. Even as the camel danced around and the neromafped snarled and lashed, Daub clung like a burr. Zarda's camel kicked the creature hard, and while it lay stunned, the man stabbed with his spear.

By the time Belon arrived, the neromafped was already dead, Zarda's spear piercing where the front of the semi-exoskeleton connected above the brain.

"Poppa," Daub called out loudly from his seat.

Belon ignored the boy and rushed to help his own father. "Is this the only one?" he asked.

Zarda tipped it over. "It's a male. So, yes."

Belon motioned to Daub. "Come here. Look at this beast."

When the boy stood between the two men, they had him kneel to touch its claws and examine its fangs. Zarda knew the boy had seen neromafped before, though he had never witnessed the ferocity of an attack, nor handled a beast that was as fresh a kill. This time, his grandfather made him study the strength and capabilities of the beast, going so far as to have the boy help gut it. Here was the perfect time to teach Daub how dangerous the neromafped was.

"Do not scratch yourself on the teeth," said Zarda. "Their saliva is toxic. You could die."

Daub tried to move away, but the men stood in the way.

"Daub," said Zarda. "You need to realize that had you been in a wagon screaming like a small child, the neromafped would have by-passed the camel, an animal too big for it to handle, and gone straight for you. You have known since birth the dangers we face every day. Yet, of late, you put us all at risk continually. Look at the size of the mouth. In a single bite, this young neromafped could have swallowed you whole. What if this were a large one, an experienced hunter? A female with cubs to feed? Who else would have died trying to save you?"

Daub buried his face in his father's robes. Zarda could see the boy's shoulders tremble, and though he felt bad, he hoped Daub finally understood the need to grow up. They mounted, and with the dead neromafped tied on behind Daub, who squeezed closer to his grandfather, rode to catch up with the troupe. On a narrow bit of hard-pan a few miles away, Maulle was lathering ointment on the gash in the camel's flank. Zarda's oldest granddaughter, who had a generous heart, laid on the camel's back, petting it and cooing softly.

"How is it?" asked Zarda, riding up.

"She lost a lot of blood," said Maulle. "We will have to split her load with the others."

The old woman didn't ask why Daub was pressed against his grandfather's back. The dead neromafped told all. While Maulle finished with the camel, Toutia cut the neromafped apart. They would not be eating dried meat that night. Both women looked up when Zarda announced they would camp on the bit of hard-pan.

"The camel will not be fit to travel for hours," said Zarda. "If she lives the night, we will be lucky."

The granddaughter stayed beside the camel, the whites of its eyes still showing. The girl pressed a bit of grain into the animal's mouth, rubbing its neck, and offering platitudes.

"It is alright," she cooed. "We are right here. I will not leave you alone."

It was a solemn evening. Zarda took time to nap, as he would be the first watch. When the fire was lit and darkness overcame the day, the family ate well on roasted neromafped.

"Grandfather," said the girl. "Why in all the old tales do they speak of the sand-dragon being an enormous beast that drops from the heavens?"

Zarda laughed. "The neromafped is a small dragon which can travel above or below the sand, but does not fly. Vicious, but of no size. There are other dragons big enough to haul away a grown elephant, and most soar as high and fast as griffins."

He called his family around the fire and told them the wondrous tales of when man first came to the land of dragons and fought against the terrible beasts that filled the sky.

In the morning, Daub stood beside his grandfather. While Zarda examined the camel, Daub said, "You were right, grandfather, I was like a baby. But no more."

Zarda studied the boy while he watched Moulle apply more ointment to the wound. There was a difference in his carriage, the set of his shoulders. Narrowing his eyes, the old man considered this change, wondering the depth of it. Daub's actions in the past had showed him unable to be responsible for even himself. Well, Zarda thought, we will see.

"Today," said Zarda, "you will ride in the cart. The injured camel will be tied alongside. It will be on you to watch how it goes. I am trusting you to tell me if the animal becomes exhausted or appears to be in trouble."

Daub looked up. His chest swelled and he nodded.

"I will ride with him also," said the granddaughter.

"No," said Zarda. "You will ride with grandmother. Daub, alone will watch."

With a haughty look at his pouting sister, the boy climbed into the wagon. It was a great honor to be entrusted by Zarda to look after one of his precious camels. Daub gave his mother a strong smile, unaware she bit her lip nervously.

"You know," whispered Moulle, "They are the only two who don't know what you are doing."

With a shrug, Zarda called out, "Everybody on top." Once in his seat, his voice rang out. "Up, my beasties, up." The camels rose, and the journey continued.

They were a day late arriving in Jadabba, where Zarda's injured son had been taken. Moulle hurried towards the inn, even as Zarda cautioned Belon about the camels.

"Not too much water at one time, particularly the injured one."

Then he followed his wife to where they found their daughter-in-law in mourning. It was not in the Rovers' way to indulge in rich displays or funerals. Their son's remains had already been cremated and two days later, Zarda pulled together the remnants of the caravan, gathering his new customers, and after hiring extra guards, headed back to the trail with his family. Eventually, they would join a larger troupe.

They were not long on the trail when Daub, who was riding atop with his mother, spotted a plume of dust in the distance.

"Mother," he said, shaking her from her doze, "another neromafped stalks us."

Struggling to rise in her seat, his mother wiped her hand across her face. "That is not a neromafped," she gasped, "but men, several men." Her eyes scanned down the caravan.

"FATHER," she shouted, "FATHER!"

But Zarad did not come. The men were getting closer. There was no time to run down the line looking for Zarda. Daub stood in the saddle and gave an ear-splitting screech, while waving his hands over his head. Many turned, but his camel, startled by both the noise and his movements, bolted. Toutia grasped at the saddle horn, trying to keep herself and the infant aboard. Daub, with nothing to grab, toppled to the ground.

The caravan tightened its ranks, flanked by guardsmen. Daub had seen this tactic before. He recognized the movements and where each rider would position themselves. Those atop hunkered down, fitting among the camel's load. Riders in the rear hustled to catch up. When the caravan finally came to a halt, the camels bearing human cargo were protected in the center of the group.

For once Daub, who would be unable to catch up with the caravan, remembered what his grandfather had told him. Instead of standing, he lay flat on the ground, tucking his head and extremities beneath his sand colored robe. Listening to the thudding hooves as they rode past, hearing the screaming war cries as the marauders circled the huddled caravan again and again, and the braying of the beasts, was terrifying. Adding to his fear, a ripple of sand shifted beneath him. Was it a neromafped? Could it hear his pounding heart? A lone tear caught in his throat, choking him and letting no other rise.

To Daub, pressed into the sand, the attack lasted for days. Even after the marauders rode away, passing so close the ground shook, Daub stayed silent. He could hear the moans of wounded men left behind, but had no idea how the battle had gone. After a long while there was silence, and the shadow of the dune above had moved to cover him. The day was waning. Daub scuttled to the top of the dune, hoping to be able to see the caravan.

From where he lay, Daub could see the bodies of three people. One was very close. Their robes were black and red. Shebbies, cutthroat desert pirates known for their grotesque cranial shape and brutality. There were also camels. Already scavengers were gathering. He could see the red and black tassels on the dead camels which belonged to the Shebbies, and further away the sky blue and tan tassels that marked those of Zadar. There was no caravan. But on the far side, creeping away between the dunes, were tracks which included the skid marks from the downed camels loads. With no time to divide, the loads were cut free and dragged behind. He knew his family would stop to regroup, but was unsure if they would search for him.

The smaller scavengers did not frighten Daub, but in the distance, he could see the V-shaped formation of Griffins. The huge flying lions could smell death on the desert wind from a hundred kilometers away.

I can't go down from here, thought Daub. I won't get across before they see me.

The griffins wouldn't care if he was dead or alive. They'd pick him off and fight for more. Edging to the side of the dune, Daub slid down. Then, with one eye on the sky, he ran around the next dune. crouching down to stay out of the open.

The griffins and the neromafped might be able to hear him, but with so much available that wouldn't fight back, perhaps they would ignore one small boy. By the time Daub had circled to the tracks, darkness was falling. The moonless night was very black. He concentrated on staying within the skid marks. If he lost his way, he would be finished.

He was thirsty and still frightened. It had taken him a long while to go the distance of two dunes from where the marauders had attacked. Suddenly, he heard a noise, a voice, softly calling. Once again, Daub dropped to the sand. Wiggling to bury himself, he hid beneath the robe. The voice came closer. He could hear sand shift away beneath the talker's feet.

"Daub?" whispered father, "Daub?" If the boy had been injured, he could be lying feet away and Belon would miss him in the darkness. "Can you hear me? Daub?"

Suddenly, from the darkness, a grasping hand rising from the sand caught Belon's ankle.

"Aaiee," he yelped, falling to the side and landing on one knee. He raised his spear, but a small voice chirped.

"Father, it is me."

Belon scooped the sand away. "Show me where you are injured."

Daub laughed. "Only where I landed."

"Shh," said Father. Holding Daub close to his side, they crept back the way he had come. When they were close to the barricade, he whistled, alerting the guards to who approached.

Toutia hugged Daub, refusing to release him even when he demanded she do so. Then her arms went slack and Daub stumbled away, grinning, her sash still in his hand. He turned to find Zarda standing stern-faced above him. The boy swallowed heavily.

"I am sorry, grandfather," he said bowing his head. "I knew yelling was bad, but you were so far away and the marauders were coming fast. Please forgive me?"

When Toutia, weeping and supported by Moulle, had collapsed at Zarda's feet, telling him Daub was missing, his heart had fallen in his chest. Their position was perilous. The marauders could return at any time. It was Zarda's decision that Belon would leave the troupe and search on foot for Daub. It was not safe, but the boy's only chance.

"There will be no moonshine tonight," said Zarda. "Be silent. Stay low. Beware the neromafped and wild desert fox. Either will consume you in a moment's time." Touching his forehead against his son's, he let the younger man go into certain danger. Three steps brought Zarda back inside the perimeter. When he turned, Belon had disappeared from sight.

Now they were both back safely, Zarda exhaled slowly, a chill running down his forearms.

"How did you find your way to us?" the old man asked.

Daub released his grip on the tether that held him to his mother. He stepped forward, stopping in front of his grandfather and meeting his eye.

"Every night," said the boy, "we sit around the fires and listen as you tell of the dangers and the beauty the desert holds. You tell us of things you have experienced, our fathers have done, and the tricks our enemies use." Daub did not lower his eyes as Zarda watched, but stayed true. "I have listened as you spoke and thought about how brave you are. You are the smartest man I know, grandfather. When I was lying on the sand alone, I remembered you telling of a wise man who hid in the bushes and one day honed a weapon from the thorns that wreaked vengeance and honor. I did not have a weapon, but I could hide. Then, after, I tracked the caravan. It was not difficult; I just followed the line of dung someone failed to collect." Daub smiled, an impish glow in his eyes. "I am thinking someone besides me should be in trouble this time."

Zarda smiled back, a rare gift from his grandfather. "Yes, I think this time we will let your squealing voice pass unnoticed. But do not think you will forever escape the dung cart." He tousled the boy's hair. "Do you think you can eat? There may be a bit of dried neromafped left."

Daub's mother came to take his hand, but he quickly avoided her grasp, his heart buoyant with pride. From behind, he heard old Zarda laugh. It was a strange but welcome sound.

THE END

The Heist

by Shawn Cowling

Wynt looked through an arrow slit in the castle wall to check the team's position. "This is not the right place," he muttered under his breath.

"You're being over cautious." Yulla, the navigator and sword-master of this merry band of treasure hunters, was not known for her patience and understanding.

Wynt understood her point. After the failure at Castle Crituca and the loss of Harina to a pit trap, cautious seemed like a positive trait. He had put the team on hiatus for the last six months, trying to move beyond the guilt of the last job. Despite being broke and hungry now, Wynt wasn't going to lose another team member because he rushed into a decision.

"Wynt is right," Deap said. The orc fumbled with a charcoal drawn map.

Wynt did not enjoy the presence of the orc, who insisted on accuracy above all else. Still, when it came to lock-picking there was no one better. Wynt thought of all the gold they were going to soon possess, and all was well.

"Deap, let it go," Hush said in an attempt to move the team beyond the current issue. The nervous elf was always one to avoid an argument within the team. "Once we get to the roof, we'll re-orient."

"I'm just saying, our map indicates a spiral stairwell should be here." Deap tapped a green finger to the map. "It's not here. This is a standard stairwell. We are not where we should be."

Hush winced, thinking Deap had said one word too many. Deap didn't really think of the others. Wynt was hopeful Yulla wouldn't react in her typical manner. For her part, Yulla took a deep breath and tried to picture her happy place—a hot spring near the northern border no one visited on account of the ghosts which frequented the waters. She had been practicing her anger management skills ever since the Forest of Rattar incident. The exercises were not helping, but her counselor and Wynt were complimenting her progress.

Once it was apparent the situation would not spiral out of control, Wynt offered a solution. "Tell you what, we've done this sort of job a hundred or so times, right? Why don't we mix it up? Those guards aren't well armed or well trained. Why don't we split up? Yulla and I will go up this way. Hush and Deap go up the other way. We'll flank the treasure! It'll be fun and new."

Not exactly cautious, but the team needed to remember how good they were at this sort of gig. Wynt glanced over the faces of the crew, hoping they were buying off on the plan. Hush stood silent as usual, and Deap picked his teeth with the tip of a blade. Yulla huffed and shook her head.

"Those guards down there aren't well trained," she said. "But the treasury room guards are Tylla

Main mercenaries, known for eating the flesh of their captives during interrogation. Anyone caught by them ends up deader than dead before they even die."

"How... how do the dead tell tales about these guards?" Wynt asked, hoping necromancy was not in play.

"It is said the band keeps a necromancer on payroll," Yulla said plainly.

Wynt cursed. He hated necromancers.

"Okay, so we're in the wrong spot and about to face down a band of mercenary cannibals with necromancy magic at the ready." Hush shook their head. "I vote we don't split up."

Deap nodded. "First smart thing you've said all day."

Wynt glared at Deap, maintaining the stare until the orc understood

"Hello?" A voice came from the bottom of the steps.

"Hush!" Wynt ordered.

"What?" Hush asked in a hushed voice.

"I mean, 'be quiet'." This was not the first time this had happened on a heist.

"Is there someone there?" the voice asked. "I heard footsteps. Or a sneeze. Honestly, I was on the other side of the door, so things were a bit muddled. If you're an evil ghost, please allow me to leave before things get weird. I'm not good with blood. Or scary things. Or gluten for that matter, but I'm not sure if that's relevant."

"It's not relevant," Deap said.

The voice screamed. Wynt, Hush, and Yulla rushed toward the voice.

"Hey, hey there...peasant-looking cook person," Wynt said in a failed attempt at being proper. "We aren't ghosts."

"And you shouldn't be afraid of ghosts anyway," Yulla added, unhelpfully.

"Who are you? The peasant-looking cook person asked.

"We're...building inspectors." Wynt flinched as soon as spoke and felt his eyes dart to the floor. He let his foot tap the stone. "This is, indeed, a building."

"Liar!" Deap shouted from high up the stairs.

"Stop listening now, Deap," Hush shouted back.

"No promises!"

Yulla rolled her eyes. "We're here to steal from the treasury. We'll spend the loot in a number of taverns throughout the region and ultimately purchase a nice cottage for each of us outside of the reach of any known officers of the court."

"Oh." The nervous woman shuffled her feet.

"What's your name?" Hush asked.

"Olanna. I'm a cook here. Hence the look."

"That's a great name," Wynt said. "I'm sure your parents are so proud of you." This line had helped him out of a few tricky situations in the past.

"They're dead." Olanna shook her head sorrowfully. "Long since. No one lives beyond 45. Grim and whatnot. And the gluten thing...Sorry. You did not need to know that. I'm nervous. First time I've happened upon a heist like this. I thought it would be different. Thought for sure I would know what to do with my hands." She was rolling her fingers in a pattern even she could not predict.

"Everything is going to be fine," Hush said reassuringly.

"Or it won't," Yulla broke in.

Olanna stepped back.

Wynt moved quickly to prevent disaster. "Olanna, how would you like to own a cottage far away from this place?" The other thieves stared daggers at him. He shrugged it off. "We need help with the mercenaries at the door of the treasury. If you can pull them away from the door, we can make off with the gold... Um, I mean, and of course we'll send for you after, so no one gets suspicious. What do you say?"

"I want 25% of the haul," Olanna answered.

Wynt's charm clearly had limits, but he admired how quickly the response came. Olanna stood before a band of potentially killer thieves—or at least Wynt liked to think they gave off a tough vibe—and a demanded a cut. She was either bored with her work, confident of her power in this moment, or just unaware of the gravity of the moment, Wynt was not sure which was more true.

"20. That's an even cut for all of us. Take it or I cut you out." Yulla flashed her favorite blade to show her true meaning.

Wynt could see the gears turning behind Olanna's eyes as she considered the counteroffer. He assumed she finally understood what her demand had meant to them, and what the fact that this band of thieves was even willing to negotiate meant for her. An opportunity. It was obvious to Wynt that she was quite smart. She reminded him of Harina. The memory was pleasant.

After a prolonged silence, Olanna nodded. "Fine."

Wynt noticed a deepening scowl on Yulla's face and broke in before blood started flowing. "Okay, we need you to get to the top of the castle and get those guards out of the way. Once the path is clear,

Hush and Deap will get into the vault and start shuffling the gold out of there. Yulla watches the right. I watch the left. Any sign of trouble and we all run, understood? No reason to get hurt or caught. We'll try again later."

They weren't the greatest instructions, nor was it the greatest plan. The whole thing had come together over a single weekend full of drinking and eating to excess. It could have been worse.

Olanna thought for a moment. "I know just the thing." She turned on her heels and headed up the stairs.

"You think one of us should go with her?" Deap asked. "What if she alerts the guards?"

"I'm not worried about her," Wynt answered. "With how quickly she agreed to help, she's been thinking of doing this on her own for a long time. Let's get to the roof."

By the time the quartet reached the roof, Olanna was already pushing a cart toward the mercenaries guarding the treasury entryway.

"She moves quickly," Hush noted. "I appreciate that hunger. Could join the crew full time."

"Let's see how this plays out first," Wynt said. "Get ready to move to the far side, Yulla. Hush, Deap, you both ready to jump?"

"I'm not a big fan of jumping," Deap said.

Olanna pushed a cart covered with food toward the guards. Wynt noted bread, cheese, berries, and a bottle of something that looked expensive. His stomach growled. He watched as Olanna was turned away. From here, he could not make out what was being said, but the mercenaries looked quite annoyed. Olanna appeared to be apologizing as she turned the cart around and made way for the dumb-waiter at the end of the walk. She looked up and, catching Wynt's eyes, winked.

Then she fell off the battlement.

Wynt nearly shot out from behind the already slim cover of the roof. His heart raced. It was Harina all over again. He watched the guards leave their posts to see what had happened to the poor cook.

"Ouch! My gods!" Olanna was shouting from the castle grounds far below. "What misfortune! Woe is me!" The guards passed looks of concern between themselves. Olanna's screams echoed throughout the castle.

"My leg! Legs! Both of them! This sort of angle is far from customary! I need aid! Guards! Guards help me! But just the guards from the battlement where I fell, they look strong and knowledgeable about field medicines!"

"That's our sign," Wynt told the team. "Move!"

Relieved that Olanna was apparently fine, the plan could go continue. Yulla ran to the far side. Deap and Hush dropped down and raced by the guards, who were running in the opposite direction.

"This is going to really affect our ranking throughout the kingdom," one of them muttered as they passed. Wynt stood watch from the roof. Olanna's shouts continued.

"I swear this pain is beyond measure! I may sound coherent, but this is purely shock that keeps my words flowing! Someone will pay dearly for this! I should say, someone else will pay dearly for this as I have obviously already paid a terrible price already!"

Deap broke into the vault before Wynt could be bothered to look away from the scene Olanna was making. Hush began bagging up the gold and tossing it out of the vault.

"It hurts no more," Olanna said, her volume dropping. "But that is surely because I am being called to the realm of the dead. Fear not for me, my kin. Should I become a ghost, I will provide you recipes lost to time. Delicious breads and desserts. Spirit cookies!"

Wynt grew worried this was no longer an act.

"It's done," Deap said all too loudly, before making an exit with bags of gold hanging off his arms, neck, and around his abdomen. Hush carried a few, too. All in all, it was a larger haul than expected.

"Away!" Wynt shouted. He readied the hooks for the team to rappel down the castle walls and off to a very wealthy future.

Several days passed before Wynt braved heading back to the castle to steal Olanna away from her life in the kitchens. He hadn't seen her since she had disappeared below the battlements, and he hoped she was not too broken to flee by carriage. He hoped she had survived the ordeal. The whole team had planned to meet far down river to disperse the loot. The time had come to ensure *everyone* was present.

Wynt wore fine, slightly used clothing, and a fancy but not too fashionable hat to hide the fact that he was very, very newly rich. He rode right through the castle gates without incident, hitched his horses to a post, and walked through without eliciting so much as a dirty glance from a castle guard. These fancy clothes were making quite the difference in his interactions with the world. It was unnerving.

He was able to walk right into the castle kitchens as well. Once inside, he saw Olanna. She was dancing around the room, dodging hanging slabs of full pigs and half cows.

"Olanna?" Wynt was shocked by the sight. "How are you doing this?"

"Wynt! Oh, I am so glad you're here. I just made a bunch of bread. Care for a loaf?"

"How are you dancing after that fall?" Wynt's face showed utter confusion.

"Oh, that? No worries. I was cursed by a witch as a child. 'Fall from four, breathe no more. Fall from ten, you'll be fine' was the curse. She was neither able to rhyme nor be threatening. Constantly falling, I am. If I fall from more than 10 inches, I turn out just fine. She didn't use units of measure when defining the spell, so natural magics just made their best guess I suppose. Not sure how the magic of the world works really..."

Wynt found himself smiling. Not long ago he had lost a great crew mate and friend to terrible fall in the middle of a job. The loss had ruined him and derailed the team for longer than it should have. Now he was talking with a courteous cursed cook impervious to perilous plunges. The world was bizarre and unfair, but the irony of this meeting could not be ignored.

"Olanna, I have your cut of the haul in this satchel right here." He tapped the bag at this side. "But I would venture to guess that you are looking for a bit more excitement than an oven and cooking for some nobles?"

It was Olanna's turn to smile now. "Are you making an offer?"

"Join my crew. Hush thoroughly likes you. Yulla has no objections. Well, regarding you on the team, that is, she has plenty of other objections. Deap doesn't speak of emotions, but we're working on that as a team."

"I will absolutely join the crew. And I will make a very tasty olive loaf to help Deap speak more freely. The secret ingredient is green olives and a lot of sugar. The buzz just makes people open up."

"I am very glad we met, Olanna."

The two snuck out of the kitchen to avoid questions, but there was one last burning question.

"Olanna, why did that witch curse you?" Wynt asked.

"Oh, well that is a terribly long, but interesting story that I can share with you on our next heist!"

THE END

A Place to Call Home

by Olyn Warfield

King Cat Sateer took in the alluring scents of magnificent flowers, as he gazed from enormous trees bearing multicolored leaves, to the sparkling greenery underfoot. Everything glowed in the warmth of a lavender sun. He watched two creatures a bit smaller than him speed by, think better of it, then turn and scamper back to address him.

Sateer gawked at the tan, brown, and black mix of smooth fur covering plump bodies held up by skinny legs. He'd never seen anything like them.

"We've been waiting for you. It's about time you got here," one of the creatures said in a tone of admonishment.

"We've got to find Trina," the other said.

They scampered away.

Sateer watched them until he could no longer make out their movement in the tall grasses. How cute, Sateer thought to himself, wondering why these lesser creatures would risk being so old. We've travelled far. A barely discernable cry for help chose our final destination. Perhaps things are worse than they first seemed.

Sateer scurried ahead of his followers. "Stay where you are. I'll be back!" he called out, peering over his shoulders, seeing the watchful eyes of his people.

He turned again and ran off, coming to an opening in the thick bushes. He went through, and his gleeful eyes took in the beautiful space, but he saw nothing to override his first impression. He turned and scampered back.

"MEOOOW! Our journey ends here!" he shouted in triumph.

"Here, Sateer?" asked Flory, his second in charge. The others froze, grasping the significance of their leader's words with perked ears.

I must keep them together. Our survival depends on it! Now, only one thing will bring them peace—a place to call home. But if I have chosen wrongly...

"Prepare to—"

Mouth open, Sateer stared over their heads. A large translucent bubble was closing in on them. It stopped abruptly, hovering before him, and Sateer watched as an opening appeared, the only occupant stepping out onto the grass. She stood upright, about 3-feet tall. Her feline qualities could not be overlooked. Wavy, shining black hair covered her entire body. She had large, almond-shaped eyes— one brown, one green—and her round face was flanked by two short, pointed ears.

The stranger tilted her head from side to side, seeming to consider the uncommon features of Sateer and his people with a graceful smile. "I'm Trina," she said, then turned to Sateer. "I know who you are. Thank you for coming, King Cat Sateer."

That voice. It's the one, Sateer thought to himself.

"Yes, it was me," she replied aloud, clearly having read his thoughts.

Sateer was startled by this intrusion. He felt his face contract into an intense, startling glare.

"We need your help," Trina said finally. "Tales of your bravery have reached us. We know of the tragedy that brought about your wandering. The great rocks that pummeled your home and forced you to flee. The sorrow and rage you all feel for those lost." Tears filled her eyes, giving proof to her stated empathy. She pulled herself erect once again, meeting Sateer's eyes and saying, "We also know what you need to heal these wounds. Join us here. A chance for a new beginning!"

Sateer eyed her intently. Sensing her sincerity, suspicions of sorcery or other trickery diminished. His expression softened. "What's going on here that would cause you to summon me?" he asked. "And how are you able to enter my thoughts?"

The cats closed in, surrounding the strange visitor. They waited in silence for her answers.

"I summoned you using a gift bestowed long ago on the rulers of Egnor. I'm the last of that bloodline, and our village is all that's left of the kingdom. I didn't know if you would hear me. Mine is only a whisper. You were so far away...I could only hope."

"That's the how. Now the why?" Sateer asked, his tone firm but not angry.

"They call themselves 'Grimites.' Their leader is called Boka." Trina said. "They came offering friendship, stating they only needed to rest before continuing their journey."

Sateer bristled. He could already assume the terrible end of the tale. "What sort of creatures are they?" He glanced around at his followers, telling them without words, "Pay attention."

She began to pace energetically, moving in aimless circles, causing the cats to give ground. "These Grimites are real mean, for starters. And they're many times your size even. They've got thick chests and four legs, but I've seen them stand on two. Hair all over, but not like mine or yours. Their hair is wiry. It sticks out everywhere. There's no softness to it. Not only that—"

"How many are they?" Sateer interrupted.

"I can't say for sure. We don't know if we've seen all of them. We tend to stay as far away from their camp as we can, and when they come to us, they come in smaller groups. They've started coming to us demanding food. If we don't have enough to give, they take what we have. It is now clear they don't plan on leaving anytime soon, if ever."

Sateer nodded. "Why would they, if they can get all they need or want here? Is there anything else we need to know?"

Pointing to her transport, Trina added, "They want to ride in the Loops. They want to control them." Her voice was bitter, angry. "But the Loops control themselves and won't let them in. Those nasty Grimites pound on them, kick them, and do anything else they can think of, without success. That drives them mad, especially the one named Boka. Would you like to take a ride, so you can see our village? Get in. All of you."

"How could we all fit in there?" Flory called out skeptically.

"You'll see."

Flory ambled over to the bubble. He peeked in before entering, cautious, eyes roving. He stepped in, turned to the others and motioned with his head for them to follow, anxious to see how they would fit. As Sateer watched from behind the group, the bubble expanded. The curious, spirited cats yowled, pushed, and tackled each other to enter as it continued to swell. Sateer and Trina entered last, then the Loop took to the sky. It lingered long enough for the cats to take in their surroundings.

"Go back down!" Sateer shouted suddenly. "Back down now, Trina!"

"What is it?" she asked, her expression showing confusion.

The cats gaped at Sateer, then searched to see what had brought about the change in his manner. Sateer could see a long dark blur headed their way. This must be these so-called Grimites.

The Loop reacted to Sateer's command, plunging back down to the forest floor. An opening large enough for all the cats to dislodge at once, appeared down its side. They scrambled out without looking back, all eyes were on their leader. Only Trina remained behind in the Loop.

"Go, Trina!" Sateer shouted. The Loop closed completely and took off at high speed. Sateer's meow rang out, "We're about to have our first visitors! Assume they aren't coming to offer friendship."

"We're ready for 'em," Flory said, bearing his fangs.

Sateer shook his head. "No, no. We'll hear them out. Let 'em have their say. Above all, follow my lead and stay calm!"

Seconds later, several shaggy creatures stampeded into view, their massive bodies and heavy steps causing the ground to quiver.

"Clear a path, before they trample us," Sateer roared. He moved away from the others, but his strategy was already in motion.

The invaders slowed as they approached the defensive cats. One of them came to the fore, his stance proud, if not completely arrogant. It glared down on Sateer.

Standing erect, eyes shifting, Sateer met the hostile stare. "Welcome friends. I'm King Cat Sateer. Come sit a spell."

Seemingly enraged by Sateer's confidence, the Grimite leader thundered, "We're not your friends! And you're not welcome here. I am Boka, leader of the Grimites, and I order you to leave this forest now!"

Sateer could see all around the raised hackles, hunched backs, and protruding teeth of his followers, as they reacted in unison to this disrespect for their leader. He knew they only awaited his command. He raised a paw. Above all, follow my lead and stay calm. He hoped those words would prove enough.

Feline tensions slowly eased, but not before the Grimite leader took notice, seemingly shocked that the cats were remaining calm.

When ferocious growls, threats, and paw slamming didn't change the cats' calm demeanor, the Grimite leader said, "We're being nice. Givin' you 'til next sunup to get away. That's when we'll be back. Be warned." He smirked pompously then turned to leave.

"Wait!" Sateer's forceful tone stopped the Grimites in their tracks. They spun around, startled by the sound. Sateer was done being a humble, peace-seeking individual. "Heed my words," he said in a low but fierce tone. "When the next sun rises, the last thing you should want is to come back to inflict harm here. If your judgement is as bad as your manners, and you do return, you'll find that we did not take your threat lightly."

Boka's dark eyes grew furious. But he said nothing. As he and his followers retreated, Sateer took note of their sluggish movements. Their lively protests had drained their energies.

"Have our scouts follow them. Find out where they came from, and how many they are," Sateer ordered Flory. The pair stood together assessing their departing adversaries.

As the sun came up, Sateer watched the Grimites boldly cross into his newly claimed territory. He'd been expecting it.

"I see you decided to be foolhardy," Sateer said calmly, once Boka was face-to-face with him.

Boka didn't say a word. He simply lunged with surprising swiftness. Sateer's speed and agility on display, he dodged the grimite's cruel attack, then leaped, landing on top of Boka, pounding and clawing at his head. Boka roared as his frenzied movements ousted Sateer, hurling the cat to the ground. Boka reared back, gathering power for a blow that sent Sateer soaring. A thick tree trunk stopped Sateer's flight.

Boka bellowed, "Bet you're ready to leave now!"

The cats stood in silence, waiting, all eyes on Sateer.

Sateer stood and shook away the pain. Let's see how tough you act when you gaze upon my true form!

Sateer sauntered towards Boka, willing his cat's body to change to something more. Sateer's bulging red eyes glittered as his lips pulled back from lengthening fangs. His stride shifted as he rose up on two feet. His chest and limbs swelled, neck tightened, dagger-like claws emerged from massive hands. Sateer quickened his pace.

Boka stood in shock for a moment, then issued a furious roar that echoed throughout the wilderness. He loped toward Sateer.

When the two hefty bodies collided, the sound was deafening. Sateer struck Boka with fists the size of small boulders. With his now-amplified strength, he pounded restlessly, driving Boka to the ground. But his enemy would not remain down for long.

Boka leaped up, snapping at Sateer with a force that could break bones. Sateer saw it coming. He dodged the forceful attack with the liquid agility of the cat within, then let out a screeching yowl as he slammed into Boka's side, sending the brute into the air. Before his enemy came to a stop, Sateer was there, striking from behind. The two fighters each attacked in rapid succession—rolling and thrashing, kicking and gouging—each delivering mighty blows.

After several exchanges, the Grimite leader began to show signs of fatigue. Boka's movements slowed. He began snorting loudly and swaying. But Sateer's pace continued until he knew his challenger could no longer resist the assault. He ended the fight with a vicious kick. Boka went down and stayed down.

Sateer turned his attention to his followers.

The individual cats were lost in a blurred melee. Kicking and biting, scratching with claws as sharp as daggers, they too had transformed. With incredible speed they avoided every attempt to grapple them. The Grimites roared in pain and frustration. One by one, their enemies retreated.

Sateer glared at the worn out, humiliated Grimites, their heads lowered, their bodies cowered in defeat. With an ear-splitting "Meowww!" he commanded his cats to disengage.

Some of the Grimites moved to gather up the wounded Boka.

"Stop!" Boka commanded, as he was being led away. He glared back at Sateer. "This isn't over..."

Sateer glared back at Boka, feeling pity for the wounded brute. "We'll be here, if you ever want to try this again. You should consider changing your ways.

He turned his back to Boka and walked away. He knew the cats had made their point. The Grimites would not return.

King Cat Sateer and his contented group lay in the sun, enjoying their surroundings, and making plans. A whizzing sound interrupted the peaceful atmosphere. The cats looked to the skies, seeing that several Loops were approaching. The strange vehicles did not set down right away. Instead, they circled slowly. Sateer could see the occupants rising inside the bubbles. They were all singing! As the Loop slowly descended, melodious, comforting sounds filled the air.

When the Loops landed, masses of Egnorians exited, still singing. They all had the same wavy hair as Trina, in several shades of brown... But Sateer noticed that only Trina had black hair. The color and the radiance cast by the purple sun set her apart from the others.

The cats jumped up. They stood wide-eyed, heads tilted, stiffing. Sateer could smell it too—food!

The Egnorians carried baskets of fresh berries, breads, green eggs, and several different sized squares and rounds, containing the delicious flavors of chicken, lamb, and their beloved fish. The cats ambled over and purred like kittens as the tasty morsels were spread out for them. The ravenous warriors ate like there was no tomorrow.

Trina, also carrying a basket, strode directly up to Sateer. Before she spoke, she offered him a small bit of fish. He accepted it.

"Thank you," he said softly.

"No, thank you. For everything." They stood together, gazing at the cats and Egnorians, all engaged in friendly conversation, like proper friends and neighbors. "We haven't sung in a long, long time," Trina said finally, "We watched the battle from above, fearing for you. Then we saw there was no need. You were amazing!"

Sateer shrugged. He felt a smile creeping over his face.

"The Grimites would have destroyed everything the Egnorians care about. They had to go. I'm sure you could feel it. It seems, they could only be driven away through battle."

"They were strong, wicked adversaries, Trina. But it was their lack of stamina that defeated them. I knew it would."

"If you say so." She shrugged. "Tell me. Have you decided to stay? You can't wander forever. You need a place to call home."

Sateer smiled, then, in a whisper, repeated those magic words, "A place to call home."

As the midday sun beamed down, Sateer was at peace—finally. He put out his paw, signaling for the food basket. His meaning was clear.

Overjoyed, Trina held out the basket.

THE END

The Crown of Laidun

by Ben Sherman

Screaming hellmetal and glowing eyes that could rent the soul threatened to overwhelm the senses of the two road weary warriors. It charged their position, and man's primal fears of mortality accompanied it. Rannon could almost smell his own fear, biting it down as he stepped to the right to give Lochlan room, trying to attack the demon on two sides. Rannon felt his eyes were tricked by some spell, as it ran at them as fast as a diving hawk. He barely managed to parry the first blow of its infernal sword; black iron meeting pattern welded steel. Had he been a lighter, weaker man, he would have been thrown off his feet. But he was a thaegar of the north.

Lochlan chanted a litany to his moon god as he swung his mace down at the fiend. As if it was a mere illusion the runic blade of the dreadknight disappeared, the fiend having spun and blocked the attack, sparks flying as its blade met Lochlan's mace. Rannon shoved his foot behind the fiend's knee, and though it felt like he kicked a mountain, the abomination staggered. Enraged, it flung its weapon's edge in a wide arc, sending both of the combatants leaping back.

Unexpectedly, it punched out with its iron fist and slammed into Rannon's stomach. The Thaegar lost his breath, and his lunch nearly met the same fate. He caught himself with his two-handed sword, sticking its point into the ground reflexively to keep himself on his feet. In his haze, Rannon saw Lochlan's mace slap into the dreadknight's shoulder, denting it but not felling the thing. Sucking in what air he could, he willed himself to grip the hilt of his sword, tearing it out of the soil. The blazing eyes within his visor grew brighter as the fiend suddenly knocked aside the mace, fumes of some unknown kind spewed forth from the openings in its horned helm. Lochlan backstepped, covering his mouth with his white surcoat. He leaped out of the way of a swing into clear air just as Rannon re-entered the fray. The thaegar swung his massive sword like an axe, it slammed between the plates of the dreadknight's neck armor, biting into what could be considered flesh. Lochlan cried in victory and leaped at the fiend to finish it, but it was his undoing. Even as the dreadknight growled like a beast from Rannon's blow, it did not falter, moving like a snake under Lochlan's attack. Rannon cried out in vain as it impaled Lochlan on the devilish sword, Lochlan's face a mask of pain.

The dreadknight tore its blade out of Lochlan's stomach and turned, swiping at Rannon to cut him across the chest. But the thaegar's iron eyes glinted with the fire of the old sagas, and he parried, the two now trading blows faster than one could conceive, moving with the instinct only gained by years of mortal combat. For a brief moment, Rannon felt as if he could win, but his sword was knocked out of his hands, and he felt a great hopelessness.

"Rannon!" Lochlan cried as the thaegar leaped back. Rannon spied Lochlan's prone form holding aloft the silver steel mace, and with his last bit of strength Lochlan tossed it into the air.

The big man moved as his life depended upon it, for it did. He spun and caught both weapons on the haft just as the dreadknight threw a blow that would have cut Rannon in two. Even then his quick thinking would not be enough, but Lochlan's god was with them, for Rannon planted his sword into the ground and caught the infernal sword's stroke with it, seeing disbelief in the fiend's hellish eyes as he raised the mace aloft. In the distance, thunder rumbled like an ancient god.

"It's just not your day," Rannon said, sending the weapon crashing down on the horned helm of the abomination. The hellmetal of its helm cried out in protest, but Rannon's corded muscles coupled with the blessed mace were too much for it. The silver steel head sundered the helm, caving it in with a satisfying finality. Unfortunately, the feeling was misleading. Even in defeat, the fiend was dangerous. It began to shudder, light glowing through every gap in its armor. Rannon stepped back, kicking the thing over and taking cover behind a log as the helm erupted like an awakened volcano, the souls of its victims along with the demon spirit residing within spewed forth in a wailing fury, threatening to grab a hold of any mortal nearby before dissipating into the nothingness of the nether.

Thunder roared once more, and for a brief moment the warrior was afraid another beast had arrived. Gathering himself, Rannon picked his way past the shriveled demon and knelt before the dying Lochlan, his broken body lay amid the bloodied soil and leaves. As the first drops of rain began to trickle from the heavens, Rannon took the warrior's hand and held it firmly, seeing there was still life in him.

"Lochlan..." Rannon breathed, not knowing what to say. He knew his traveling companion was a dead man, and he would not dishonor him by lying. But even the fatalistic thaegar was heavyhearted in this moment.

"Looks like you'll have to go it alone." Lochlan replied weakly, trying in vain to squeeze Rannon's hand back. "Fear not for me! Fear not. I will be well. You must take care, Rannon. Here..." Shakily, Lochlan's other hand reached into his surcoat and produced a vial of glowing silver in liquid form. Rannon was taken aback, unsure of what to make of the sacred oil, but he took it at Lochlan's request all the same.

"These lands are ever perilous. Your blade might need such a boon..." He coughed. "Take it and lay me under this tree with all my things save...save thus." He said, and Rannon saw he was fading. The warrior could barely swallow, and his eyes began to glaze.

"Farewell, Lochlan. May you see your ancestors in paradise." Rannon said. Lochlan replied with a small smile. "Farewell, Rannon Brycefalk, for I go to the halls of Limradil, into whose company I shall now no longer be ashamed. Farewell..."

The rain now battered down upon them, steam rising from the dreadknight's ruined armor. Even under the shade of the oak tree, it matted the thaegar's hair, hiding what one might claim were tears. He stayed there for a moment, watching the droplets splash and bounce atop his companion's form. He wondered what the point was, and why he was once again burying another friend.

It had been two days since he had left the dreadknight in ruin. Two days of drudging through muck and woodland. Two days alone with his thoughts. Even for one so young, they could turn grim. Upon his shoulder, the dreadknight's hollow helm hung loosely, Rannon's weregild for his friend's demise. He thought of the War Cleric, recalling their conversations about the land he walked. Lochlan had once claimed this was boar country, but Rannon had not seen hide nor hair of any beast larger than a cony, and so he had to eat what little rations were left. He felt it was Alfrikr's providence when he met the merchant named Garland on the road. The man talked a lot and said very little, but he did tell Rannon less than a day's travel ahead was the Barony of Laidun, where he might yet again pick up the trail of his quarry.

The forest grew sparse, leaving plenty of room among the trees. The area had likely been cultivated over the last few generations. Rannon found Laidun as the sun began to crest over the horizon of the afternoon. It was a settlement that seemed to insist upon its own opulence with the short walls and the gate made of fine timber, and with statues of stone depicting the likeness of their southern gods. Within the walls, save what had to be the baron's manor and a few shops, everything else seemed made of poorly constructed wooden homes. He had never seen such a small-town attempt to be so grand.

He strode through the gate, immediately gathering looks from passersby and the men on watch. Rannon only gave them a glance, his gait never slowing. The thaegar simply made his way through the first street, one of the few in Laidun unhindered by an errand or a day job. He wished to pray to Alfrikr for wisdom, or Rálda to ferry Lochlan's spirit safely to the shores of the upper realms, but found no temple or shrine for any gods he recognized this far south. Soon he found something else he was looking for, a place to get a drink. He had been south of the Dragonback long enough to know the soft taprooms by the shape of the structure. This one had a rectangular sign that bore the mark of the ox hanging over the street.

Inside, the torches gave the common room a warm quality, day laborers and local women cavorting and enjoying conversation as someone laughed in a high-pitched squeal. Some spoke in hushed whispers, likely discussing the wars in the west. Rannon leaned against the counter, ordering a mug of mead and paying for it with the toss of two pennings, trying to drown out the mutterings of the others so he could enjoy his drink. He had little interest in news or fretting over the world. His life as a mercenary was harrowing enough.

He heard the mad laughter again, causing the mercenary to growl in annoyance. He took his drink and veritably inhaled the brew before he turned to see who was disturbing the atmosphere. Weeks of hard travel and the death of a friend at the hands of a demon, he simply wished to ensconce himself in drink! He turned, iron eyes sweeping the crowd to find the source before his gaze fell upon the man whom he had sought these past months.

Axel Lambrey sat at the far end of the common room, howling in his strange howl as he tried to tell the tavern maid another story. Rannon would usually be considerate of the awkwardness placed on the woman, but he was a hound that had found his quarry. Immediately, he stood up and left the counter, his eyes glinting like silver in the torchlight. Axel saw the tall, foreboding predatory thaegar approaching, the sniveling weasel performing a classic double take.

"You..." He sputtered, looking around for a way out. Rannon continued forward like a landslide. The death of a friend at the hands of a demon had left him drained and enraged, and Axel shoved the girl aside and grabbed his chair, tossing it at Rannon like an unwieldy axe. Rannon caught the chair, and to the amazement of the crowd he tore it apart in one brutal move: chair legs and splinters flying. The wiry man gaped as his table was overturned by Rannon with ease. Axel was struck across the chest by a chair leg Rannon had thought to keep, sending him back against the wall.

"Please! Galena's mercy!" Axel coughed as much as cried, knowing he was beaten. With men under his command and fully armored, he could be imposing, but caught alone in a bar? Rannon was disgusted just looking at him. He was about to strike again, before the big man felt the cold blade of a sword touch the base of his chin. It was followed by four other points at his back, and a rough voice saying, 'come with us.'

Rannon obliged. It was a small comfort to see Axel taken into custody as well.

Despite the structures around the estate, the manor itself was impressive. If Rannon had awoken within the chamber he was currently in and was told that he was in Andred City, he might have believed it. The stone hall was well carved and laden with tapestries and the furniture upholstery looked as soft as the posh southerners that mumbled to one another as they watched him.

Upon a raised seat sat a dark haired, slightly overweight man in robes that attempted to have royal dignity. Before him were four men bearing spears and clad in chainmail hauberks, though no other guardsman stood near Rannon. Once they had discovered the nature of the helm he had upon his back, they kept themselves more than a few paces away from the northerner. Before the baron spoke, he noticed a younger woman in a dress, peering at him from the back of the hall like a mouse peeking out of a hole.

"Hail, thaegar! It surprises me that one such as yourself has come upon Laidun." The ruler said grandly. "I know that war and monsters are what your people seek, and they are far to the west."

"Vengeance as well, my lord." Rannon replied, inclining his head slightly, as he had been taught to do years ago.

"I see..." The baron replied thoughtfully, placing a hand on his mouth to consider. "Forgive me, I have not introduced myself. I am Gaspberg, the regent of this barony until my niece reaches her majority and assumes the position. You, as you've told my guards, are Rannon Brycefalk. Tell me of that helm you carry. Its very sight offends me and my men, though I fear to know its true origin."

"It belonged to a Dagfyrtu." Rannon began, which brought looks of raised eyebrows and confused faces around the hall. Rannon tried to find the right word in the common tongue. "A... a Dreadknight from the Realm of Hell."

Gasps erupted from all sides, and Rannon simply glanced at those retainers who watched, daring them to call him a liar. The young woman, most likely the niece now that Rannon considered it, looked at him in a strange way. She looked with interest, but not in a salacious fashion. He did not think he liked it, and he continued. "It was not three days north of here on the main road, halfway between here and Valcy."

"You slew such a fiend?" Gaspberg said, clearly thinking such a thing impossible. Even the spearmen at his front seemed either disturbed or simply filled with disbelief.

"Not alone, my...I had a friend who aided me. He perished in the battle. This helmet-" He began, hefting the thing. "-Is my weregild. Recompense for the loss of him, and a trophy of the battle."

"I am grieved to hear of your loss," the lord said, though his mind seemed far away. An unarmored dreadknight was more than a match for any five men, and dreadknights were never without armor. It was by fate that he managed to survive the encounter, much less kill the wretched thing. "But why did you come to my fair town?"

"I am looking for the man you dragged me from. He is called Axel, and he knows where I might find the one whom I truly seek. The one who is responsible for the death of my thaegar comrades. It is why I traveled south, my lord. He is Marius

Haukenbrek, General of Dysax. A man who betrays his allies and makes pacts with demons."

If the name was known, no one gave any sign. It pained Rannon, but he had begun to expect such disappointment wherever he went. Marius was clearly not as noteworthy as he had tried to appear in the army. The lord brought him back to the current conversation.

"In your land, you follow the law. In this land we do as well. And you have committed damages without recompense. In that we are agreed?"

"Yes," Rannon said simply. What he said was true, it had been dishonorable to attack so recklessly, even when justified. Even if he would do it again.

"What if I told you, not only could you repay your debt, but make some money for yourself?" Gaspberg offered. "In fact, I will aid you threefold. Perform a task for me, and I will give you this man, Axel, provided you do not murder him. That is against our law."

It was Rannon's turn to be taken aback, half expecting to be put in chains once the baron had finished his questions. "What would you ask of me?"

"Your people are troll slayers. We have a troll that has been eating my caravan guards and stealing trade from here for over a year. We call it the Trollking. Kill it, and you will be paid and allowed access to this... Axel. And you may take what gold that you will from its hoard, though only what you may carry."

"Why do you call it the Trollking?" Rannon asked, which brought a laugh from Gaspberg. Clearly, he had been expecting Rannon to be perturbed rather than intrigued.

"Because it wears a crown, and it is said to be the smartest of its kind."

Rannon was escorted to his quarters by a flank of guards, having been given leave to stay the night to cleanse himself and tend his wounds and aches. He had been on the road far longer than a few days. The warrior only wished Lochlan had made it far enough to rest and eat heartily too. Though as he pondered it, he supposed his friend's feast and sleep in the halls of the heavens made his own pale in comparison. He found he simply wished Lochlan was here to speak with and joke as he used to. With a will, Rannon pushed the thoughts away, expelling air out of his nostrils.

The manor was large enough to dwarf many of the thane's estates, but in the southern lands, it was quite small. Most Andredian or Vrettonian villas were as large or larger, and even in the spartan conditions of his people, a Jarl's home could likely match it. They turned a corner in the stone corridor, and Rannon leaped back in surprise to see the girl from the hall suddenly there. He reasoned it was due to her knowing the estate far better than he.

"Sir Brycefalk, may I speak with you?" She asked him, and without waiting for his answer, she glanced at the guards and indicated they leave. The men hesitated, looking at one another until she crossed her arms and gave them a look, and they exited quietly. She began to walk, obviously expecting him to follow. Rannon figured as long as it was going to his room, he did not care overly much.

"What do you wish to speak to me of, my lady?" He asked her, trying to remain polite. Lochlan, and truth be told everyone he had known personally, had criticized his abruptness towards others. Learning courtesy was a difficult measure. He halted in the hall, suddenly deciding he would rather get whatever topic it was over with before he made it to his room. He did not trust himself to not fall asleep on the spot. Even now, he felt bleary eyed.

To his surprise, she blushed.

"I'm sorry, sir." The girl said. "I simply just want to speak without interruption. You see I... well so few of your people come down here from the mountains..."

"I'm confused." He admitted.

"Your language," she clarified, her eyes brightening. He crossed his arms to listen. "It's fascinating. I'm the only person here in Laidun interested in etymology or...anything outside of its walls, and as you can imagine, I've not traveled much. You speak Drimgoth, do you not?"

Rannon snorted, amused at the topic. He was so tired anything would seem funny to him. "That is my mother tongue, though we're raised with the common speech as well."

The young woman wiggled in glee, her eyes alight. "It is the first true language of men, back when there was naught but Dragons and Dwarves, and the Giants roamed the land in great droves!" She told him breathlessly, missing the contradiction of her statement. Rannon did understand what she meant, having heard the old tales from his clan, and she was not wrong. All three ruled the world at one point, until the Conflict of Dwarves and Giants, and the War of Skyflame. "Oh, please teach me some of your tongue!"

"I'm only going to be here for one night," He thought aloud. "Two or three if I survive."

She opened her mouth to speak, only to immediately deflate, looking dejected and embarrassed. The girl bit her lip. "I'm so sorry. I should have been more thoughtful on things." He could tell she had a good heart just from her manner and he felt a pang of guilt for denying such a rare person a simple enough request. "I know you've just lost a friend and you're about to battle a troll and–"

He held his hand up to interrupt her. "I would be happy to teach you some of my language," he assured her, to her flustered delight. "I am Rannon Brycefalk, it's good to meet you. Who are you?"

"Yes, um..." She gave a curtsey, and to his surprise she went from a flustered girl to a figure of regal bearing like it was second nature. Perhaps it was, he thought. "I am Niemessa, niece of the regent."

Rannon was not surprised, but it was still a bit strange to know he was speaking to nobility so casually. Was he even supposed to be speaking to her?

"And future Baroness." He said to her, and she seemed embarrassed again. She grabbed his arm and led him down the hall, presumably to his room.

"Once my uncle deems it time, yes." She admitted, before changing the subject to what was truly on her mind. "Now Rannon, what does... dagfyrtu mean? Is it an accurate translation of dreadknight?"

"Not entirely," He explained, trying to recall his old lessons from adolescence. "Dag means knight or elite warrior, but Fyrtu is more akin to horror or fear. No, terror. So 'Knight of Terror' is probably the best translation."

"So that's the etymology?" She pondered as they halted before a great oaken door. She popped up, smiling. "Here we are! Your room, I have been told. But I would love to know one or two more words?"

Rannon desperately wanted to enter the room, but she had been hospitable, and he found he could not refuse a pretty woman. Even less so when tired.

"Stald," he said after a moment's thought.

"Stald?" She echoed curiously.

"Property," he explained, running his hand over the doorway's stonework. "Something you should know, as future baroness. Laidunstald, one might call it, for you'll inherit it one day."

The hunters had led him as far as the river.

The wilderness was thick with tree, rock, and upturned earth, and had Rannon not known better, he would have thought this was part of the great Blackwood. From what the Laidun huntsmarshal had told him before they left, the troll had only been a nuisance the last year. Had the thaegar been told differently, he would have thought the beast itself would have kept the forest as preserved as it was. He loathed trolls, but sometimes the stupid brutes could be inadvertently useful. Unfortunately, this was not one of those times. Rannon was left on the eastern side of the stream, the three hunters not daring to enter troll territory.

Grim of visage, he knelt down before the tree line, listening patiently. The sun was past noon, but there were many hours yet of daylight. The birds he heard were few in number upon the eastern shore, and he saw little in the way of boar or deer paths through the brush. Carefully, he crept northward until he found a large indentation in the ferns, a broken sapling strewn across the roots of another like a loved one clutching a casualty of war. Even a brown bear did not lumber around like that.

He followed the ruin and crushed foliage for a time, but the path would have gone cold by the reckoning of most men. To a thaegar it was clear as day. Rannon could smell the troll. A musky scent, stuffy and old like an abandoned cellar. A cellar that was filled with chests stuffed with corpses and pig dung. It grew more unpleasant the further he walked, until he found what he was looking for. The land grew rocky, and the maw of a cave emerged into view, menacing the landscape.

Curiously, Rannon saw no bones before the mouth of the cave. The tracks and the smell were unmistakable, but it was not lost on him how unusually tidy the area was. He chalked it down to the monster arriving only recently. Glancing around, he realized the wildlife had gone from sparse to silent. He took off his sword belt, placing the scabbard on the ground softly before he drew his large sword. It was a troll-slaying weapon, made to rival a troll's simian reach and robust enough to hack and pierce its tough flesh. He would need it unbound and on hand in case of an attack.

Briefly he contemplated his options. Normally, he would stride out into the clearing and call out the beast, goading it to leave its cave. Trolls were weakened in the light of day and generally dumb enough not to care. If this one was smart, however, all that would do is warn the troll it was being hunted. No, he would leave and make camp upwind of the thing, and attack at night when it least expected it.

And so, he did, making camp a mile away and eating what rations he had, cold. As the sun began to set, he still did not make a fire. His night vision needed to be perfect. One missed sign of the beast's whereabouts would lead to his death, for trolls were brutal abominations. Many thaegars had wound up in the bellies of monsters they themselves hunted; such was the way of things.

Once night had truly fallen, the bugs began to chirp around him, shielding the sound of his soft footfalls as he stalked like a wolf back to the mouth of the cavern. The moon glared upon the ground, its pale light reaching a few paces into the cave. Rannon had to trust the Gods as he walked the breadth of the light, before he entered into shadow bearing the dread steel of his sword.

Inside, the cavern was dry, but there was a very wet smell within. A smell different from the troll. It reminded him of when he was a boy, when his father had taken him hunting bear when he came of age. It was the same smell as the elk they had found, its chest having been broken open by the beast's immense strength. Briefly, Rannon wondered how his path to vengeance had led him here, and how many would have died without justice if he were to fall in this foreboding place. He would make sure that did not happen.

Through the dark, he moved, his sword as close to his body as possible. The silence was deafening to the warrior, every step like an audible clap to his ears. He did not know how far he walked before he heard the deep rumble of the thing's breathing within the next chamber. The smell was far more rancid than it had been previously, almost more than he could bear. Somehow, the troll had caught whiff of him.

There was a sudden change in the heavy breathing, followed by the sound of tumbling stones as it began to move. Rannon backed into a crevasse, holding his breath and keeping his body as still as the stone. One by one, the tread of heavy feet drew nearer, a horrific growl emanating from the darkness as a massive shape passed by Rannon's position. It blotted out what little light he had to go by, but the warrior knew now was the time to strike.

Rannon stepped out into the main tunnel, expelling a lungful of air the troll immediately caught the scent of, and though it spun like a whip, it was not fast enough. Rannon honed every muscle in his powerful form and shoved his blade into the beast's midsection. It gave a harsh, guttural cry so inhuman it froze the blood in Rannon's veins. The blow he had delivered would have felled a horse, but the monster still had life in it. The troll, paralyzed for only a moment, whipped around, tearing the sword's hilt from Rannon's grasp. As it moved, it swung an arm the width of a log. Rannon ducked and dived, the limb slamming into the stone like a sledgehammer. Rannon hit the ground, clipping his head on a rock, a sharp pain blossomed in his head but he had no time to assess the damage. He continued his graceless roll until he hit the next wall. The troll punched in his direction, but it miscalculated how low to the ground Rannon was, and its fist cracked into the rock above Rannon's head. Without pause, Rannon pulled his seax from his boot, embedding the blade into the troll's meaty forearm. It reeled back and squealed, giving Rannon time to regain his feet and yank his sword out of the thing's side.

The two stumbled back from one another to better see their foe, to Rannon it showed some cunning truly did reside in this thing's head. Any other troll would have still been enraged, likely caving in the tunnel around them with its thrashing. But this one gave him a cold look of unnatural intelligence, and Rannon saw the glint of the crown that lay upon its head. Wounded though it was, a troll was as resilient as stone, and Rannon was running out of ideas. The beast snarled, raising its massive fist to strike. Rannon lifted his sword, but the expected punch was not coming. Instead, the troll shoulder rushed him, and just before Rannon was hit, he saw what he believed to be a grin on the monster's face. He saw white, and Rannon could barely feel when he hit the ground; one small consolation before he was hit, he felt his sword slide into the beast yet again. The troll could take more than a few hits, however Rannon could not.

It was a testament to his will that the thaegar could move at all, swiping with his sword and striking flesh again, though with little strength behind the blow. He saw a flash of his surroundings; the jagged rocks, his body on the floor, the troll raising its fist for a blow that was coming, one that would not be a feint. Rannon rolled like mad, the blow meant to crush his ribcage, cracking stone as it hit the floor. He grabbed at his sword hilt once more, and even as the troll reared back, Rannon rose with it, placing his point beneath the monster's chin and shoving it upwards, sliding through meat and bone into the thing's small brain with all the strength he could muster. His arm shuddered when it hit the back of its skull, unable to penetrate past the thick cranium but doing its damage, regardless. The troll's body shuddered; Rannon leapt away before the massive body fell on top of him. The only sounds given by the troll as it hit the ground was a loud 'thump' and the air escaping its lips, followed by the crown clanging against the ground.

Rannon breathed heavily, groggy and bleeding in more than a few places, but alive. He realized at that moment that he had not truly expected to survive. The slaying of a troll alone was a task for only the best of thaegar warriors. He did not know if he should feel lucky or proud, but at the moment all he felt was tired and satisfied the task was done. The warrior yanked his sword out of the dead thing's skull before he retrieved his seax.

It was then he had the fright of his life. Rannon felt the cold grip of horror in his chest when the troll raised its punctured head slowly. Somehow, the crown had not rolled off the thing but stuck to it like glue. As Rannon took the hilt of his sword and backtracked to get room to swing, he heard a terrible rattle in the beast's throat, and its eyes fixed on Rannon. They were glowing with a pale light.

"Leave this place, troll slayer." The troll said, as if he had not just been slain by Rannon. The fact it came alive again nearly made Rannon forget that trolls could barely speak, and none spoke with a voice so haunting and fair. "You cannot win here.

Laidun is mine, for my vengeance is nigh. Run, or you will die."

"What the hell are you?" Rannon asked faintly. He felt his resolve returning, but he did not know what other witchcraft lay ahead. The troll, or whatever was controlling it, looked at him with a baleful gaze.

"I am the bane of Laidun." It replied. "The wrath of the dead. All who serve the usurper will die."

Rannon had heard enough. Whatever this thing was, it was a restless thing that needed to be killed. The thaegar wielded his sword, the heavy blade lifting high above his head as the troll began to move. It lifted itself with surprising speed, its arm reaching for him. Rannon was one second too quick for it, but as it had moved, his sword missed the felling stroke. Instead, the blade hit the crown, hammering against it. A preternatural force kept it stuck to the troll's head for but after a moment Rannon's strength won out, batting it down to clatter against the stone. Immediately the huge troll lost the witchlight of its eyes and slumped, falling like a sack of rocks, dead.

Rannon looked between the crown and the now motionless troll, suspicious for a few moments until he was certain it would not get up again. With that, he knelt down and began to cut the troll's neck in small strokes with his seax, severing the spinal cord and muscle tissue so he might take the head back as proof of his deed. Once done, there was a brief snap as he used his great muscles to break the troll's bones within the neck. Rannon took the head by what scraggly hair it had and went to grab the crown as another trophy. When his hand gripped the gilded item, he felt a small shift of wind, and a low moan escaping from further within the tunnel, as if the cavern were itself a beast.

The man did not have time to do more than react in surprise before the cavern shrieked. A scream that threatened to deafen him erupted through the stone, and Rannon cried out in surprise and despair as he felt all of his fears and anxiety surface in his mind. All he could do was let go of the crown and cover his ears, clumsily sliding his sword under his arm as he ran for his life. No longer was he the fierce warrior that had faced a troll or a dreadknight in combat. He was a frightened boy, unable to break free from a depression that engulfed his mind and tore at his will power until he stumbled out of the cavern mouth, reeling weakly until he dropped onto the ground, losing consciousness, and fading into oblivion.

He hoped whatever lay within did not pursue him, or he would not wake up again.

The new sun's warmth at his back, Rannon sat on the log, smelling the mixture as it was boiling in the pot. His muscles ached, but he felt far better now that he knew what he was dealing with. His wounds cleaned and patched up, he gingerly pulled out the silver liquid Lochlan had given him, pouring it in the pot, a plume of pungent, copperish smell followed that he could taste in the air. He hoped he could apply it to his blade like he could any other oil of slaying. The dark liquid coalesced into a brew the color akin to a full moon upon a clear sky. Rannon noticed there was even a light glow to the liquid as he stirred it.

He removed the pot from the fire and let it cool, ladling the brew onto the oil cloth and coating the blade. The liquid granted it a sheen of silver as he wiped it across the blade, he gasped at the beauty of its gleam. Gripping the hilt, he flipped the blade and made sure the oil coated the entirety of the steel before he got to his feet, the warrior swinging the sword in slow, deliberate swings to make sure it did not slide off the sword. Satisfied, he set his sword down and placed ripped fabric in his ears, making small noises to make sure it blotted out all noise. Rannon had heard tales of wraiths that used their wails as weapons, his elders calling such aberrations 'banshees'. If last night's scream was any indication, that was what he faced.

With the sun still over the land, Rannon trekked once more into the cavern, finding the troll's corpse just where he left it. The head lay slumped beside its body, but there was no crown. Rannon knelt down and ran his hands over the floor, unable to see that anything had come or gone through here. Were it a true beast, it might have gnawed on the corpse or make some signs of its passing. As far as he reckoned, nothing had been moved save the crown.

Not able to hear his own movements, he stalked forward extra carefully, keeping his sword at the ready and his footfalls soft. The darkness in the passageway engulfed him, the light that emanated from his blade by the oil was his only saving grace. As of yet, there was no hint of the crown, or the malicious spirit within. All he could hear was the beat of his own heart, and he had the fear that whatever lay within could do the same. He had walked twenty paces past the corpse of the troll before he began to see light again. A soft light, but illuminating, nonetheless.

Grimly, he stepped into a roughly hewed dome chamber, a small sliver of light peering into the back of the cavern. Within the light, Rannon caught the glimpse of something shining like gold. No, the thaegar sucked in a breath as he peeked in; it was trove of gold! Piles of gold and silver lay against the walls. Rannon's eyes drank in the riches, the slayer almost losing his concentration before he spied what he sought: the bejeweled crown.

For a brief moment, he believed he had truly been undetected, but he was proven wrong in short order. Rannon grunted when he felt a frigidness fly up his spine, suddenly stricken by an attack he couldn't see! Paralyzed, he was blown off his feet by a scream that tore into his mind just like the last one. This time he had steeled himself, however. Reeling, he hit the back wall and briefly saw a glimpse of a waifish form hovering closer, reaching out with sharpened claws. He swiped out with his two-handed sword, hitting something less than real but undeniably there. Immediately, the banshee shrieked again, this time in pain.

In a whirl, the restless dead clawed at him, fingers sliding past the skin of his flesh to cut at his very soul. The sensation was indescribable, uninhibited pain that lay past what his mind could fathom. Somehow, he felt the truest part of his inner being was wounded. He shuddered violently, but managed to hold himself firm, opening his eyes and seeing the banshee in full view. He did not know if it was unable to remain invisible any longer due to weakness from his blow, or if some connection had passed into him from her own strike. Either way, it made no immediate difference to him as he shoved off the wall, Rannon's sword leading into a savage diagonal blow that cut the aberration in two. Her form rigid, gleaming cracks of white light shimmered down her form ubiquitously before bursting with a blaze of brilliance; the banshee falling onto her back, her ethereal form shifting between this life and the next.

Rannon approached its form, his iron eyes glinting with abhorrence at this mockery of nature. The warrior flipped his sword in a backhanded grip, pressing his palm upon the butt of the hilt to shove the blade into her ghastly body to end the fallen spirit's pitiful existence.

"Rannon Brycefalk...I bid thee listen!" He heard echoing in his mind. Rannon hesitated, shocked at the sudden message that pierced his thoughts. Briefly, his stubborn nature nearly took hold. This was an undead monster! He should slay it as he did all inhuman beasts. However, something halted his coup de grace. To his surprise, the message was not filled with fearful pleading, but sorrow and anxiousness. "Slay me now, and you shall never find whom you seek."

"What does a spirit have to say to me?" He demanded in a growl, unable to keep the distrust from his voice. "You, who have stayed in this world when it was your place to fade into the realm beyond? Do you beg for another moment of this cave before you pass on with naught but useless tricks?"

Her form shimmered, and she stared dead into his eyes as she spoke her next words, her voice ghastly and brimming with volition: "I cannot be released until I wreak vengeance on the one who wronged me." A mournful woe escaped her. "Grant me this boon, if not for my sake, then for the sake of my daughter who yet lives. Of all I have come across, you, Rannon Brycefalk, would know the pain of losing the ones you love. And the need for justice."

Rannon stared at her ethereal form in abject confusion, caution warring with instinct. Had her words not given him a vague reminder of a story about Laidun's Lady he had recently heard, and had she not known his name, he might not have listened. Could she be Niemessa's mother? Slowly, Rannon pulled his blade away from her, stepping back to grant the ghost the chance to speak without fear.

"Speak, spirit. And tell no lies, lest I banish you from this plane." He warned, sword outstretched threateningly.

It had been two days since Rannon had left the foul cavern with the head of the troll in his possession. Once the warrior had presented it before the regent, Gaspberg, the entire town was in an uproar. Women thanked him and flirted idly whilst men asked how he had performed such a deed, some folks even offering their daughter's hands in marriage. Rannon spoke little of it when pressed, trusting in his visible weariness to keep further questions from assailing him. That night he had slept like a log, having found his conversation with the banshee illuminating enough that he needn't worry about his next move. Once awakened, he had been told

Axel Lambrey had fallen ill with the plague. Rannon had taken it with difficulty, wishing to see some proof of his ailments. He was provided with a cloth of blood they claimed came from Axel's incessant coughing. He decided to take it as fact for now and distracted himself by spending the rest of his day speaking with Niemessa, making her day, and causing her to positively bubble up with his knowledge of Drimgoth.

The following day saw the banquet hall alight by torch-fire, the evening's festivities underway. Richly burnished oak tables were set in ranked file down the width of the broad hall, a carpet rolled out down the middle which led to the stairs that brought one up to the Baron's table situated upon a platform for all to see. Servants waded through the crowd, bringing the newly seated guests their refreshments, having just placed down the boar and turkeys they were allowed to cut into. Businessmen, homeowners, even travelers were allowed into the hall during the celebration of the troll slaying, as much in an open statement of safe roads as it was a feast to congratulate the hero of Laidun.

Now Rannon sat in the great hall's foyer, a cloth sack in his hands as he awaited on his cue. The tall warrior's mouth watered from the food, but he had gone days without food before. He could wait a few more minutes, instead wondering once again if this was all some trick. Had he given his trust too freely? She was an undead abomination, but was it so different than speaking to his ancestors? Lochlan's oil had worked on her, but that did not mean she was evil at heart. Only that her means of remaining was unnatural. No, he would follow his instincts. Axel had become unavailable, just as she had warned. He was going to do as he had been bid.

Through the oaken door, he could hear little. But no doubt the Baron Regent had given a grand speech and perhaps even a toast before Niemessa went to get Rannon, opening the door to poke her head out. The normally grim thaegar couldn't help but smile. Yesterday had been a good day, chiefly thanks to her. He had never seen anyone as effervescent as she was, and so enthusiastic about his culture. For a moment, he even forgot about what he was about to do.

"It's time!" She said, holding the door open for him.

Rannon got to his feet, letting her present him with a flourish of her hands. She seemed to love making a scene. Rannon felt a bit embarrassed, and Gaspberg gave a nod to Rannon in acknowledgement, smiling to the feasters who had grown silent at the sight of the thaegar. The baron looked so pleased. Soon he would not be.

"And here he is! The troll slayer!" Gaspberg declared, and almost all at once, the crowd rose and clapped. Some hooted and howled as others looked on with interest; a few of the women particularly. Men raised their mugs as the baron did, and under different circumstances, Rannon would have felt truly honored. No, he did feel honored. He had killed the beast, after all. Instead of bowing, he held his hand up, letting the crowd calm and be seated once more, showing he intended to speak. Niemessa and her uncle watched him, slowing their claps with the crowd until all was silent.

"I am not worthy of this praise. It was a job that I am paid amply for by your generous host. In my land, trolls haunt the mountain passes and lurk in the deeps all around us. Hunting them is what is needed, and so I did only what was needed for this town." Rannon said, and he presented what he held close to his breast. A small item under a sack of cloth, undoing the covering to reveal what lay within. "But the troll was not your only danger, I am afraid. Often times, dangers appear in places you least expect them. What I did with the troll was needed. What I do now is not for money, or for myself. I simply will do what is right."

Murmurs began filtering through the pregnant silence. A few of the drunker crowd laughed as if he had given a hilarious anecdote. They sobered up quickly when the brilliance of the crown he carried gleamed from the torchlight shimmering off of it. Every sapphire on the gilded crown glinted in this hall once again.. Someone dropped a glass, the tinkling of something shattering was given no attention as everyone gazed upon the artifact. A hefty woman gasped, and a man pushed his chair back and rose, but said nothing. Rannon looked at the baron, Gaspberg's mouth opening and closing, not finding the words to add for many moments.

"The crown!" He exclaimed in bewilderment. Rannon saw the fear in his eyes. "It cannot be! Wh– Where did you find that!?"

Rannon ignored him. Rather, he turned to Niemessa, who stood a few steps above him, their eyes on level with one another. Gingerly, he presented the treasure to her, placing it before her with his upraised palms. "Do you recognize this crown?" He asked her gently, reading her expression. Though they were the same age, at that moment she seemed very young.

"I do...It was my mothers." She said softly, confused.

"Do you trust me?" He asked her, his tone steady. She did not speak, but slowly she gave him a nod. He smiled at her. "Then allow me to place it on your head, my lady."

"Sir Brycefalk, answer me!" Gaspberg demanded, attempting not to appear too domineering.

Again, if Rannon heard him, he gave no sign. She nodded to him, licking her lips. Rannon set the crown atop Niemessa's head, the object fitting perfectly on her waves of dark hair. Immediately she gasped, and it pained Rannon to see her falling forward. Rannon caught her in his big arms as the crowd wailed, hoping beyond hope he was right about trusting the ghost. He could only imagine the images flashing through her mind at that very moment. Niemessa clung to him and whimpered, but she did not take the crown off. He saw tears begin to stream down her cheeks.

"Guards!" Gaspberg cried at the scene. He pointed at Rannon avidly. "He's attacking the lady Niemessa! A-Arrest this man!"

Hesitating only a moment, the wards of the hall rushed toward them, their swords still half sheathed before Niemessa cried out with volition. Rannon blinked, looking very much like the hound dog on the floor, its head tilted in wonder.

"No! Do not touch Rannon. It is my uncle you will apprehend!" She ordered, suddenly standing on her own two feet. Even Rannon was surprised at the strength in her eyes, and he stepped down the stairs, giving her room. Her gaze swept over the assembly of civilians now slack jawed at their tables. To see her mother's death before her eyes, she handled it very well. Gaspberg broke the silence, laughing incredulously.

"You are not yet fit to rule, dear niece. Nor have you given a reason for my arrest." He said, shaking his head pitifully and taking a step toward her. "You still have much to learn, I see. Now...hand me that crown. We must find out how this vagabond acquired it."

"By the order of your baroness, you will arrest him for the murder of my mother!" She declared. The guardsmen looked absolutely awestruck at what was happening. Rannon simply crossed his arms as fear and denial leaped into Gaspberg's face.

"What baseless claims!?" He extorted, huffing. "I know not how this...this trickster has found the crown of your mother, but by what right do you accuse me of slaying her?"

"These are all too true, as you well know." She told him, tears still brimming her eyes as she looked at him. It was clear to Rannon that she had looked up to the man. She turned to Rannon, holding out a hand to him. He took it, knowing it was a sign that he might speak. Gaspberg snorted and ordered the guards arrest Rannon once more. No one moved.

"The crown and her body were within the troll's cave. Along with a knife in her back, coated with poison..." Rannon produced the knife from within his knapsack. He let it sit on his palm so that all might see. On it, something wet had rusted the tip, and the closest guardsman whispered, 'the baron's knife!' The crowd was still in shocked silence before it was broken by a harsh sound from behind Rannon.

"Unfortunately for you..." Gaspberg said, his tone changing radically. There was a small 'slip' sound as he drew out a dagger, and Rannon turned in time to see the unbridled hatred in his eyes. If the banshee had told the truth, and Gaspberg was in league with Haukenbrek, there was a good chance this man's evil had led the dreadknight to these lands. "I have a second knife!"

He struck like a viper, moving quicker than the thaegar might have expected to his credit. However, Rannon wasn't one to be dispatched like that. He raised his forearm to halt the downward stroke of Gaspberg's arm, simultaneously grabbing the man's thin neck and shoving him onto the stairwell in front of all, banging his head on the stone. Gaspberg's knife dropped from his nerveless fingers.

"I've fought demons and trolls, and you think you'll be the one to kill me?" Rannon remarked darkly, and he began to squeeze Gaspberg's neck until the man fell unconscious. Rannon released him to tumble down the small flight of stairs, hitting the ground in a heap. Immediately the armsmen went to gather him up, taking the baron to the dungeons on Niemessa's order. Rannon looked at him, and the thaegar felt broken inside. Broken in spirit, robbed of his revenge. Eyes glistening, Niemessa watched her uncle go, coldly. When she turned to regard Rannon, even through the moisture in her eyes, she saw confusion.

"What's wrong?" She asked.

Rannon could not answer for many moments, and when he did, he needed all of his strength to drag it out.

"I can't continue down this path of revenge." He declared softly. All of these people died due to the Lady's revenge on Gasperb, rightful as it was. Had Lochlan's death been his fault? It was his journey, his cause, that had brought him here. Perhaps he should go back north to his home and live as men do. "I won't."

It was a statement of finalization, and he turned to place his hand on Niemessa's shoulder.

"Your mother told me she was proud of you." He said to her, and she looked at him in awe. "She may rest peacefully now, I think. Now that you're here to take her place."

"You..." Niemessa said, clearing her throat. She tried to regain her dignity, though she always had that tinge of girlishness to her when speaking to him. "You have saved Laidun from a terrible troll and... brought me closure. How may I ever repay you?" Her dainty hands grabbed his, holding them close as the crowd in the hall cheered at Niemessa taking the mantle of baroness, reciting her name for all to hear.

"For the troll, I merely ask to eat well, sleep well, and have some time with your uncle to find out just what he wanted Axel to keep secret to his grave." Rannon said, and for the first time in years, he seemed young as well. His eyes brightened as they looked at one another. "And for the latter? That is reward enough."

At that, Niemessa stood up on her tiptoes and kissed his cheek. "Then let's eat, and maybe after you can teach me a few more words?"

THE END

Sunset of the Wolf

by Richard Reydan

The howl of wolves could be heard outside of the ger. It was the call of friends, beckoning Attaces to his next journey. Tonight, he would join his ancestors on the great ride into eternity. First, however, a successor had to be chosen, a task that had thus far proven difficult.

Inside, the old Qayan rose up from his pillow. The smell of cooked goat pervading the air had awoken him from his slumber. Above his bed in the candlelight knelt his wife, dabbing his blooded mouth with a cloth. She reached forward and placed a second pillow tenderly under his back and grabbed a bowl, offering him to drink. He took several strained but welcome sips of the fermented horse milk.

Attaces's weak body lay diminishing upon the hard, wool filled mattress in the center of the ger. He struggled to eat or drink. Instead, he stared at the wooden door of his hut, waiting patiently. The ger itself had been his home since his marriage to his beautiful and attentive Khumoo. This place had been his life, gifted to him by his father, Tundrek Two Eagles—also once Qayan of the Khamag Gol.

"We have so many memories here," he said, coughing.

"Memories to last another lifetime, my little wolf-ka."

It was the pet name Khumoo had used for him since before they were married. Bending forth, she kissed his forehead and took the bowl of milk from him, placing it next to a small stove at the foot of the bed.

"Do you remember the first time you came through that door as my betrothed?" asked Attaces.

"How could I not remember, my wolf-ka," replied Khumoo, smiling. "You kept me up all night!"

Attaces laughed. "And that was just talking about the lone wolf I had seen on the plain."

The effort made him cough, and he could feel the blood rising from his chest. His wife instinctively held the cloth out for him as he spat. It was red, as it had been since the moons were last full in the night sky.

Attaces and Khumoo held each other's hands and laughed at the memory, their old eyes connecting, absorbed in their deep love for one another. He had made love to his wife for the first time here, in this same ger, and it was here that she had given birth to his two sons. It was also here where he'd been chosen to become Qayan of the Khamag Gol.

His life was rooted in this place. It would be hard to rise free.

Soon he would be naming the new chieftain of the tribe. He continued to look through the two center posts, or the "gateway to the stars" as it was named, which framed the entrance. Outside, the call of the wolves was replaced by a shrill wind that tried to pierce through the thick, hide-covered hut. He turned to Khumoo as she placed another piece of dried dung onto the stove. It turned a deep red and took flame, generating heat to help fight off the chill of winter.

"You still need much rest," said Khumoo. "You should not have called your sons this night."

"The council of elders could not choose. Therefore, it is to the ancestors that we must listen." He said this, not as Qayan of the Khamag Gol, but as their spirit guide. He alone could commune with the ancestors and receive visions from them. "The circle of life must be complete before I pass." Attaces wheezed as he spoke. "The next qayan must be chosen tonight, and I must make the right choice."

Khumoo wiped away more red spittle from him, then placed a small pot onto the stove. After a moment she ladled some of its contents into a bowl which she offered her husband.

"Come, you must try to eat."

He managed to mouth a small, but still boned, piece of meat. The flesh came away easily in his mouth and he sucked on the marrow within. After he had finished, he spat the small, now meatless goat bone back into the bowl Khumoo held before him. The old qayan once again smiled upon his wife.

"Can you remember when we first met?"

"How can I not?" Khumoo dropped a bloodied cloth on the floor. "You were hunting."

"Yes, yes that was it," said Attaces, again coughing. His mind wandered in remembrance. "It was out by the northern hills. I was trying to blood my first eagle, but it would not come back."

"And I was walking back to show my father a newborn goat I had found."

"And the eagle I was calling swooped down and snatched it from your hands."

"I never did see that goat again."

"Nor I the eagle."

Outside, a great wind whipped up once more, battering the ger, and Attaces turned to the door again. Khumoo offered him more milk.

"He comes," said the old qayan.

The sound of horse hooves could be heard approaching, holding sway over the wind until the clattering steps halted on the hard, frosted ground.

"Hold the dogs!" A voice said over the tumult, giving the traditional visitors greeting.

The qayan made an effort to raise himself from his bed, but a gentle hand stopped him.

"You are not strong enough," said Khumoo.

"I am qayan," Attaces argued. The alcohol had awakened some fire within him. "I should rise and show strength, especially to my sons."

"You have been qayan and father for many seasons," his wife said reassuringly. "You have shown strength and honor throughout that time. You have met with the elders today, so you have no one to impress anymore. Your sons will still honor their qayan." She placed a gentle hand on his shoulder. "Now you can rest."

Attaces did as he was told. His eyes followed Khumoo as she rose from her kneeling position and opened the door. As she did so, a strong gust entered, threatening to knock her over. Candles flickered, becoming engorged, growing brighter than before, casting dark shapes about the ger.

Almost instantly, the wind ceased as a huge figure filled the doorway. The man bent low to enter the hut, throwing a long shadow over the prostrate Attaces. The new arrival wore a thick coat of hanak skin, over which he'd thrown a heavy wolf pelt. As he removed a round wolf-fur cap, a flow of long black hair fell to his shoulders. Muscular hands brushed straight a small, virgin beard.

"Jarl-ka!" Khumoo drew her son into her bosom.

This only emphasized the man's size—Khumoo was short, barely making the warrior's waist, and she could not embrace him wholly. Before going to kneel before his father, Jarl turned to his left and gave reverence at the altar of the gods. His eyes, however, fixated upon a spear that was attached to a support pole above the altar. This was the spear of Tundrek Two Eagles, and it had been in the tribe for as long as anyone could remember, passed down from qayan to qayan.

The young warrior turned to his father's side. "I raced Handor here, and I beat him again, Father. That is now six races in a row. He cannot beat me with neither horse, axe, nor spear. I am a man." He beamed.

"You are indeed a champion," said Attaces. This is how he shows his age, thought the old man, in boastful outbursts. "But hair upon the lip does not a man make."

"Qayan, he's only showing you how proud he is." Khumoo had always favored their younger son, Attaces knew, even to the resentment of the elder brother.

"I am sorry, Father. You are right. A man must show respect for his brother." Jarl turned to his mother, a huge grin upon his face. She had returned to the side of the bed. "Wait till he arrives," continued Jarl. "He will be angry again." The young warrior and Khumoo laughed, but Attaces remained stoic.

The qayan signaled that he wished for more drink, and Khumoo held the bowl for him. He drank deeply, hoping to imbue as much of the drink's power as possible. He could feel the alcohol stir within him, awaking his limbs. As qayan, he had one final task to do, and in that he must be strong.

The sound of more horse hooves came from outside, thundering across the ground. A disgruntled rider dismounted and uttered a curse. "Mag the whore...Bah! Hold the dogs."

Khumoo moved to the wooden door of the ger. As she untied the lock, the winter wind blew in again, this time covering the altar with dust from the barren plain. The candles again threatened to blow out, as in stepped—

"Handor-ka!" As before, Khumoo embraced the new arrival. This time she was able to fully enclose the visitor in her arms.

The new visitor repeated the ritual, kneeling before the altar, his eyes closed as he mouthed a silent prayer. He then rose and rounded upon Jarl.

"You cheated!" Handor glared at his brother, who grinned back in defiance. Handor roared with anger, looking up at his younger but much larger brother. "You tied my horse's feet together! You could have broken my mare!"

Jarl stood his ground, as if encouraging Handor to strike him. A reproachful look from Attaces silenced them both. The younger brother responded by kneeling by the bed.

"I am sorry brother," said Jarl.

"Kneel Handor," Khumoo said firmly. "And take off your cap."

Handor removed his cap as requested, though he refused to kneel. Unlike Jarl, this warrior wore his hair short, in the fashion of the veterans.

"I am sorry father." There was genuine remorse in Handor's voice. "I meant no disrespect, but you cannot let this go unpunished." He pointed at Jarl, "He says he is a man, but he acts like a youngling."

Attaces looked to Handor. "He has apologized to you Handor and...he has assured me it will not happen again."

"When I become qayan, he will need to show true respect," Handor said through gritted teeth. "Else I will send him into the high mountains of Nemed to drink hanak piss and live with the goats where he belongs!"

"Handor!" Khumoo scowled at her elder son.

Jarl, still kneeling next to his father, looked from Handor to Khumoo and then to his father. The young warrior's face became taut as the candles flamed up stronger than before, lighting up the ger.

"Stop this!" commanded Attaces. "Tonight, you and your brother must put aside any and all quarrels that you have, and you must listen to me."

"I will honor you, Father," said Jarl. "And I will honor my elder brother." He loomed over his father and patted the old man on the arm. The gesture was both affectionate and strong.

"Handor, kneel before your qayan." Attaces glared at his son. "Although you are eldest, it does not give you right to stand before your chieftain."

Handor knelt, refusing to make eye contact with either his father or his brother.

When all was quiet, Attaces spoke. "Today, I met with the council of elders to choose which of you should be the next qayan." He coughed again, and Khumoo attended to him. "A decision was not made—"

"But Jarl is a boy!" shouted Handor. "Surely the elders could not follow him?"

Attaces ignored his son's outburst. "It is now I, alone, who must choose between you. There can only be one qayan, one who protects the tribe throughout the harsh winters on the great steppes and defends his people in war. A qayan must be as indomitable as a pregnant hanak facing a starving bear. He must be as cunning as the winter fox, if he is to deal with the other tribes. Lastly, a qayan must have the courage of a wolf. His tribe must believe in him, and they must be willing to die for him."

Outside, the howling of wolves could be heard again, rising over the wind as it rolled across the plain. The chieftain looked to his sons, both kneeling close together on his right. He could feel the anger still billowing in Handor, but his eldest remained silent. The youngest now looked calm and reflective, though Attaces knew what Handor had said about Jarl was true. He was young and immature, though he had unmatched potential, and a great fire burned within him. Every day Jarl grew bigger and stronger, even now he could defeat almost any man in wrestling. His skill with the spear was unequaled, and he could hit a target further than anyone with a bow. The younglings warmed to him, often gathering around him to watch him wrestle and run alongside him as he rode out to hunt.

Most of the tribal elders however, liked Handor, for he represented the old ways and traditions. His horsemanship and warrior skills were good, but he had always been quick to boredom. Even as a child he was not be able to endure long training in the skills of the warrior without wanting to do something else. This lack of focus had caused many arguments. The greater skill he carried over his younger brother, however, was his acumen for strategy, for warfare of the grander scale.

At that moment Attaces convulsed once again, Khumoo moved to hold her cloth out to him but the qayan refused. "They are calling me. My time is short." The howling intensified as Attaces looked over his sons. "We must seek guidance from the ancestors. You must listen to me, not as your qayan, but as your spirit guide."

Attaces lay back, upright against his pillow, and asked for more milk. This time it was Handor who held the cup for him. The qayan signaled to Khumoo to pass him his spirit bundle that lay upon the altar. She returned with a large, rolled blanket containing the items that enabled him to commune with the warriors and maidens of the past.

"We must listen to those who lead the way before us," Attaces said. "Their spirits will aid us in the decision."

Attaces unrolled the bundle before him. On the blanket lay an assortment of small bones, an eagle feather, and a necklace of wolf teeth which Attaces placed around his neck. Next, he picked up a small leather bag from which he withdrew a handful of ash, tossing it upon the fire at the foot of the bed. A swirl of smoke and flame arose around them, and the candles in the hut blew out, leaving only the fire to give them light. Shadows frolicked across the ceiling and the sides of the ger.

The sons of Attaces looked on. They had seen this many times before, and from the eager look in their eyes, Attaces knew they waited for him to begin the Song of Tears. Opposite them, Khumoo crossed her arms over her chest in reverence as she followed the shadows dancing above her.

Breathing deep, Attaces let out a rolling guttural sound. At first the chanting was low, emanating from his throat until it burst out of his mouth. The voice moved around the ger, as a wind swirling amongst rocks. He threw more ash upon the fire pit and swayed as he sang his song, awaiting the ancestors' response. He jolted once, then twice, and his eyes rolled to the back of his head. He began to shake as he opened the void to the plain of the ancestors.

His song continued.

Before Attaces lay The Great Steppes. He was surrounded by a pack of wolves, howling at his arrival. They moved forward and rubbed against his legs. He welcomed them and looked to the glowing stars. The entranced sprit guide now opened his eyes again and held one hand up, pointing to the roof of the ger. Various shapes of an incongruous form circled above them as the fire flickered below. A baying of wolves seemed to echo within the ger.

Almost imperceptibly, the howling began to recede to a whisper as a hundred voices took its place, resonating about the ger and gaining in strength. The voices grew louder, both male and female, in a cacophony of noise. Finally, the voices coalesced, a hundred all saying the same words. Against this backdrop, Attaces continued his guttural song as his wife and sons looked above them. An image appeared in the flickering light, showing the shadow of a lone man walking amongst the mountains.

"Once," began a Hundred Voices, "the Winter Wind and the Summer Sun argued about which was the more powerful. The Winter Wind could blow and freeze a man to death. It could knock over a ger and bring down terrible snows. The Summer Sun, however, could burn a man to death and crack the very earth beneath his feet. It could dry out all the lakes, and no animal can live without water."

Attaces threw more ash upon the fire as the shadows flowed and flickered about the hut. A Hundred Voices continued its parable.

"The Winter Wind and Summer Sun quarreled when they saw a man walking the Steppes. A shawl of the thickest wolf skin wrapped his body, and a cap of the warmest Hanak fur covered his head."

"It is no good quarrelling," said the Winter Wind. "Let us put our power to the test and see if we can shake off this man's covering that he wraps around him. I will blow the man's shawl off, and so you will see my power."

The Winter Wind began to blow hard, twice knocking the man to the ground. But the more the Wind blew, the tighter the man wrapped the shawl around himself, bending into the gale. The Wind finally gave up.

The Summer Sun took his turn, rising high up in the sky, moving the clouds out of the way and shining bright upon the shawled man. As the man walked further, the Summer Sun shone even brighter, its heat biting down until the man removed his shawl and quenched a great thirst from a water bag.

"See," said the Summer Sun boastfully. "I am strongest."

The Summer Sun was now a blinding ball of fire. The grassland around the man took flame, and he was surrounded by a conflagration. After a short moment, a charred and smoking skeleton collapsed upon the ground. The man was no more.

The image above the ger disappeared, but the shadows continued to dance, flowing around those witnessing the spectacle before them.

Attaces stopped his song and coughed. "The story has meaning for you both." He gazed at his sons, a mystified look upon their faces. "One of you is the Winter Wind and the other is the Summer Sun." Attaces turned to Handor, "Which one are you?"

For a moment, Handor appeared in thought and an idea seemed to come upon him, but he shook his head. "Father, the story could have many meanings."

"What then, is your response Jarl?"

All eyes turned to the young warrior, who also looked deep in thought. A grin appeared upon his face and he spoke. "The ancestors tell us that the Summer Sun is strongest. It won the contest, forcing the man to bend to its will and take off his shawl. Thus, I am the Summer Sun for I am strongest, and so the tribe will bend to my will."

"What say you Handor? Is your brother to be qayan?" asked Attaces.

A despondent Handor rose as the shadows continued to swirl above his head in the shimmering light. "My brother is correct father, he is the Sun. I am then, the Wind that flits and fleets. Even as a child, I blew everywhere and argued with all, which is why I am called Handor Locks-With-Horns."

"So, I am to be qayan?" Jarl now rose, his eyes wide and his face beaming with pride.

"No," replied Attaces.

"What?" Jarl glowered. "But the ancestors..."

"Have sent us a vision. You have given an answer, but you have not understood the wisdom."

Jarl huffed and walked to the Altar. Khumoo moved to hold him back.

"Leave him," said Attaces.

"If you will not choose me to be qayan"—anger rose in Jarl's voice—"then I invoke the Challenge of the Spear."

At that moment, the swirling shadows within the ger moved with speed, shaking the altar. Above, the Spear of Tundrek fell before Jarl's feet.

"So be it," said Attaces. "The ancestors agree."

The qayan jolted again as a fit of coughing overcame him. A sliver of blood trickled out of the corner of his mouth. Only the soft presence of Khumoo by his side calmed the seizure.

"What must we do, Father?" asked Handor.

Attaces indicated for Jarl to stand before Handor. "You must each take hold of the spear and wrestle it free from the other. He who secures the spear will be qayan."

At this, a confident Jarl smiled and gripped hold of the spear, holding it in front of him.

"But beware," warned Attaces. "The spear must not break, for he who breaks the spear of Two Eagles can never become qayan." Attaces motioned for Khumoo to raise his pillow again so that he could sit fully upright.

Handor also grabbed hold of the spear. Both brothers now looked at each other, both tightening their grips upon the oaken shaft. The shadows moved above them with increased intensity as the brothers began to twist and turn the spear against each other. The weapon creaked as it was lowered for a moment, each combatant turning to pivot the spear to their own end. Jarl moved to push the spear forward and downward, using all of his weight and height. Handor pushed up, the effort telling upon his face. Slowly, Handor was driven to his knees as Jarl forced the spear above Handor's head.

In a last effort, Handor used his strong knees to resist the overpowering Jarl, but the spear began to creak and bend. Handor let go of the shaft and collapsed onto his knees in front of his brother. Jarl stood tall, the spear still in his hands, a look of triumph upon his face.

The young warrior raised the weapon above his head and roared, 'I am qayan!'

As he did so, his massive arms bulged, his grip tightened upon the shaft, and it splintered in two. Around the ger, the shadows warped into a frenzied dance. A hundred voices hissed and howled as the shadows swirled together and forward, passing into Jarl and vanishing. The force of the shadows knocked him onto his back. The fire dwindled, and the candles flickered back into life.

All was silent for a moment. Even the wind outside seemed to have frozen in time.

Handor moved forward and picked up the two shafts of the spear. He looked in disbelief to his father and then to Jarl, who was now rising from the floor. A look of shock also settled on the young warrior's face.

"The Challenge of the Spear is over," said Attaces.

"What does this mean, qayan?" asked Khumoo, who moved to aid Jarl in standing.

"It means that fate has decided," Attaces replied. "Handor Locks-With-Horns is to be qayan."

Without another word, Jarl deflected his mother's grip, shoved passed Handor, and went out of the ger into the winter night. Handor moved to follow his brother.

"Leave him, Handor," said Attaces. "Let the wind cool his anger."

"I am confused, Father." Handor was examining the pieces of the spear in his hands. "It all happened so quickly."

"Yes, Handor," said Attaces. "But it is the will of the ancestors." His breathing was shallow as he spoke again. "Now I will ask you again, do you know the wisdom of the Summer Sun and the Winter Wind?'

Handor looked at his father and then his mother. Finally, an answer seemed to dawn on him. "Although the Sun was the strongest, it did not know when to stop and thus destroyed what it was trying to help."

Attaces smiled. "Well done, my son." His face then turned stern once again. "Now you know why you must be qayan and your brother must not. He would give our people strength and they would be mighty over all the tribes. But I fear, if he were to become chieftain, he would lead the tribes into the greatest danger they have ever faced. Every Alanii tribe would catch fire and our children would burn." Attaces took a deep breath. "You must become a strong leader, Handor Locks-With-Horns. You must unite all the tribes behind you...you must prepare them for when Jarl returns. When he does, you must make him your subutai. As your general he may find peace. Promise me that you will do everything to make sure that your brother never becomes qayan."

Handor rested the spear blade upon his father's bed and reached to his side, drawing out a small dagger. "With this blood so I swear." Handor cut into the palm of his hand.

Handor moved to wrap his bleeding hand, but Attaces motioned to him to take up the spearhead once again.

"H...hold it," the old man said, his voice fading. "Become the qayan for all our people. Keep them safe, especially your mother."

Attaces looked to Khumoo, knowing his time was short. His breathing labored for a moment, then he turned back to Handor.

"I, Attaces Speaks-with-Wolves, do give you the spear of our fathers." He gulped for air and spoke again. "This day, the spear of Tundrek Two-Eagles is no more." His chest wheezed but he called upon as much strength as he could muster. "Today...the spear will hold a new name, and as I die, my spirit will enter this blade, and it will bare my name."

He convulsed again. This time, Khumoo was unable to reach him and a large globule of blood exploded out of his mouth, covering his bed.

Attaces looked at his wife, her grey hair belied the shimmering blackness that it once had, though it was still long and plaited, the same as it had been since he had known her. Fifty seasons had passed since they had first met, yet she still had those deep hazel eyes he had fallen in love with. Even now he would have wrestled the fiercest bear or hunted the quickest pantara for her. She may have aged, thought Attaces, but her beauty is still beyond compare.

Khumoo moved to Attaces and mopped his mouth with a fresh cloth. Blood had begun to pour freely. "I will send Handor out, you need to rest my wolf-ka."

"No, let him stay." His old voice was low and garbled as he tried to clear his mouth. "Stay Handor, as I did when my father passed. And Khumoo, you must call him 'Qayan' now, for the circle of life begins again." Attaces looked up to the center of the ger, a small sliver of light had begun to break through the vent in the dome. "What time is it?"

"The light is fading, Father," said Handor, his face sullen. "The day's hunt is over, and the eagles will be returning to their nests."

"Khumoo, my eternal love, take your morin khuur and play me out of this life."

Khumoo rose as commanded and took the horse-head fiddle and bow from the altar. She looked at her husband, smiling, tears welling in her eyes as she began to play. The sound of the fiddle vibrated softly around the ger.

"Lead me to the Plains Where the Horses Run," said Attaces.

His eyes closed, and he felt himself lift. He was once again a young boy in the hills, and in front of him, he saw a young girl with a small goat in her arms. As Attaces held out his arm an eagle came to sit upon it. The young Khumoo stood beside him and gave him her hand. Attaces took it gently, looking over the long grassy plains where a herd of horses grazed.

As they walked, a warm sun set orange on the horizon.

THE END

Tanri

by Elana Gomel

Every five hours, Tanri growls, and I silently beg him not to stop.

His growl reverberates over the valley like a distant thunder, and my father stands still, his hand over his brow, staring into the glassy blueness of the sky, as if he could see the shaggy dog-head rising over the horizon like a storm cloud. But there is nothing. Just the fresh leaves of the beach trees in the small wood nearby, so piercingly green they look like a handful of emeralds. And the white and purple anemones peeking through the last year's mulch. And the new shoots of wheat in our field, as tender as my baby sister.

And the growl of a titanic dog that shakes my bones like ague, as if I were Nana's age.

My mother calls me in, and I go back into the kitchen reluctantly. She is sitting at the scrubbed table, cradling Hayat in her arms. The baby's rosy face is peeking out from her swaddling.

"Look, Yildiz, she is smiling!"

I obediently bend over the baby. Yes, indeed, she is smiling—a sweet toothless grin. I chuck her under her fat chin, playing the role of the adoring elder sister. And all the time, a part of me is standing aside from the scene, observing it with a detached and superior coldness. I see my mother, the farmer's wife, in her hand-embroidered blouse and full linen skirt, the Sunday meal spreading the delicious aroma of a roast through the house. I see my father, the farmer himself, coming into the kitchen and bowing to the icon in the corner before embracing his wife and the baby. And I see myself, the eldest daughter of the house, curtsy to my father as he plants a perfunctory kiss on the baby's forehead.

And the growl of a giant, invisible dog punctuating our idyllic existence every five hours. The growl comes from outside our valley.

My name, Yildiz, rhymes with the word for the star, because I was born at night, just as my sister Hayat was born at high noon. Her eyes are blue, and mine are black—black as the sky dome that presided over my birth, the single star at the zenith like a silver nail driven into the night. I think my parents had hoped starlight would filter into my soul and illuminate it, dispersing the dark. They were wrong. The night has colored my mind, and even the friendly rainbow sun rolling over the blue sky cannot chase it away.

I start setting the table for supper.

"How long will it go on?" my mother asks. "The baby can't settle."

"It will soon be over, Nur," my father says. "Thunderstorms never last for more than three days."

I know I should keep my mouth shut but I cannot help myself. "Thunderstorm?" I ask. "The sun is out!"

I point to the low-hanging orb in the sky, pearly-pink, and juicy-red, and butter-yellow, shining with the colors of peace and contentment, filling our valley with warm light.

My mother looks at me with irritation. "You know how it is, Yildiz," she says. "We always have dry thunder for a couple of days until it starts raining."

"Until Umar blesses us with rain," my father corrects her gently.

He is a devout man, and it is his duty as the head of the family to keep us happy, kind, and faithful. The rest of the valley inhabitants look up to him. If he says that the growling of Tanri is dry thunderstorms, they will accept it.

I nod, putting the roast and a loaf of home-baked bread onto the table. Settling the baby into her basket, my mother gets up to pour a small beer.

And all the while, the giant wolf-dog growls beyond the deceptive azure of the sky. And I know that one day he will never stop until the sky shatters in slivers of blue glass and sets me free.

There are a hundred and fifty households spread through the valley. My future husband will be a son of one of them. Most families have many children—Udmur and Umar have blessed us with abundance, opening the wombs of cows, ewes, and women. Our family is the exception. Two daughters only: one almost fully grown, one a baby. One morose, one joyful. One dark, one light.

For a long time, I had been the only child, my parents' shame, my mother's secret sorrow. I had seen my mother's tears when she sat by the fire, late into the night, her lips moving as she prayed to Umar and her twin Udmur to bless her with fertility. I had seen my father's furtive glances as he tried to measure my budding beauty and translate it into a dowry. At least, in this one particular aspect, I am not a disappointment to my parents. My mirror tells me I am as straight and slim as an aspen tree, and my skin is as white as its bark, though my hair and my eyes are as black as the shadow-filled Thorny Wood. I am different from other girls my age, and therefore desirable in my own way.

Unfortunately, my valley is so small that the sons of the wealthiest households cannot consider me just an alluring stranger. They all know me; or they all know about me– my dark moods; my flares of anger; the stories of my kicking a dog and abandoning a lamb in the pasture. And they have all heard rumor of my sneaking out at night to wander in forbidden places near the Thorny Wood.

But my father is not concerned. The young men and women of the valley do not have many choices. Sooner or later, somebody is bound to knock on our door bearing a bottle of cider, a honey cake, and a cloth embroidered by his mother or his sister, to ask for my hand in marriage.

On that day, I will say "no".

Tanri has stopped growling, and the rain my father promised has come. The crystal dome has clouded with a yellowish patina, like skin on fresh milk. A gentle downpour is making the leaves glisten, the fresh grass sparkle, and my sister laugh. My mother is holding Hayat in her arms, showing her the silver droplets coursing down the windowpane. When she sees me skulking in the corner, she calls me over. Her voice changes subtly when she talks to me as opposed to my sister. She thinks I don't notice it, but I do.

"Come, Yildiz," she says. "Let's watch the rain together and give praise to Udmur."

I come over reluctantly and stare at the sky-dome. When it rains, it seems even closer, so I can feel its weight on my shoulders.

"Where is the sun?" I ask.

My mother sighs.

"Come on, Yildiz," she says in a pained voice that I know so well. "You know where the sun is. I taught you this when you were your sister's age." She smiles at Hayat. "You know that when Udmur brings harvest rain, he leaves the sun in the keeping of Hadis, his brother, behind the Thorny Wood so it can shine again next morning."

I remember the questions I peppered my mother with when I heard this story; the questions to which she had no answer and which she finally cut short with an irritated shrug. The questions remain, but I no longer bother voicing them.

If the sun is hidden, why is there light? If Udmur gives us rain to grow crops, why can't he destroy the Thorny Wood that hems in our valley, so we will have more arable land?

And the one which always elicited the blankest of all stares. If the sun is put away, why is the star still in the sky?

This night, I wait till my parents fall asleep and tiptoe toward the front door. My eyes are dark-adapted; I find my way unerringly in the murk-filled passage. As I go, I hear a gurgle. I stop and retrace my steps, sneaking softly into Hayat's room. Now that she is one year old, she sleeps alone.

I lean over her cradle. My sister is awake. I can see the wet gleam of her open eyes in the blackness of her room. But she is not crying. She is lying quietly in the dark, making strange cooing sounds.

"Hello, Hayat," I whisper to her. "I'm your big sister."

Another gurgle. Can she even see me? Why wouldn't our parents leave an oil lamp in her room? Their ostensible reason is fear of fire, but I know better. They want her to sleep through the interval of darkness, to plunge into unconsciousness and never to wake up until the multicolored lantern of the sun rolls up the dome of the sky. They want her to be unaware of the night – and of the silver star that anchors it.

"Little sister, little sister," I murmur.

How vulnerable she is, here, in the dark, all alone! In the dark that is like transparent gauze to me.

I see myself picking a pillow from the rocking chair in the corner, lowering it gently over her round smiling face. She would feel no pain. It would be like going to sleep. And the next morning, I will be, once again, the only daughter of the Rafat household. The only daughter – and the only heir...

"Little sister, do you want to see the star?"

She gurgles affirmatively.

I pull aside the curtain that my mother has drawn. The night in the valley is quiet and velvety-soft. Large moths flit across the windowpane, their wings the same color as my hair. The shadows in the orchard weave together into a tapestry of sly expectation. There is no light coming from the outside except for the metallic glow shed by the star. It is both faint and harsh.

I take Hayat in my arms and bring her to the window.

"See, little sister," I say, pointing at the silvery disk. "Yildiz, the star. My star. The one that shines at night. Always there, always in its place. Holding up the dome of heaven."

Hayat smiles.

I put her back on her cot and slip out of the farmhouse. Outside the fields lie silvered by starlight, like the old broken swords Demir keeps in his barn. I was not supposed to see them, but I snuck in there once with a boy named Safet, who was the closest thing I ever had to a friend. The swords belonged to the old bad time before Umar and Udmur took us under their protection. There were all kinds of rumors about them, but when Safet and I first saw them, we were disappointed. The shards did not look like much: just slivers of corroded metal, dull and heavy. But I could not stop thinking about them, so I snuck into the barn again later, alone.

I walk across the fields, wading through the puddles of shadow, clutching a sword–shard. When I swiped it, I counted on Demir not knowing how many he had, and indeed, he never noticing a piece was missing. Swords are supposed to be graceful and sharp, but these ones are broken into jagged pieces, as if they had been shattered against something much harder than themselves. Though, what could be harder than steel, I have no idea. Individual shards are useless: dull and randomly shaped, with no handles, impossible to wield properly. I tried to make a wooden handle for mine, but the wood would not mate with the metal, as if they hated each other. Eventually, I simply wound a piece of cloth around one end, so I could hold it without cutting my hand. And even so, I feel the cloth straining away from the shard, almost as if it were alive and repelled by the alienness of the steel.

A mournful howl echoes through the night and I stop, listening. Is it Tanri again?

Tanri is a children's tale, outgrown by all of my former playmates. Outgrown by everybody but myself. A shaggy dog with burning red eyes, he is supposed to prowl the edges of the Thorny Wood at night, threatening the bad boys and girls who would not sleep peacefully in their sturdy farmhouses behind the drawn curtain, protected by the icons of Udmur and Umar. He is a story told by exhausted mothers at the end of the day, as their offspring burrow deep under the warm bedclothes, a delicious shivery warning.

But I know he is real. I have seen his predatory face limned in shadows against the rainy sky. I have heard his voice in the squalls of thunder.

I am straining my ears, but the howling dies down, and I realize it is Demir's guard dog, perhaps sensing my passing by. I am a shadow at night, a danger, and a challenge. A lawbreaker.

I come to the edge of the Thorny Wood, where gnarled trunks and arthritic branches twine to create an impassable barrier. No leaf ever graces their hard blackness. No flower ever peeps from between their swollen roots. No pall of green ever veils their uncompromising ugliness. And yet the trees are not dead; they grow hardier and taller every year, reaching toward the dome of the sky, scraping it with crooked thorns. Children are prohibited from coming close to its edge. Adults know to stay away without such prohibition.

A claw of a twig scratches my cheek. I pull out the sword-shard and hack at the barrier. The shard bounces off the hardwood and the clumsy cloth swaddling I put around it slides off. The jagged edge bites into my palm, drawing blood.

Suddenly, with a painful creaking and straining, the knotted branches withdraw, making a narrow twisting passage.

I stand still. Is it really happening? Is the Wood reacting to my challenge? Or is my desperation making me see things that are not there? The fear that the passage might suddenly disappear breaks my paralysis. I press through, holding my wounded hand aloft, letting drops of blood fall onto the wood—black upon black. My hand is burning, and I will it to burn more, to match the excitement that is setting my brain on fire. The thorns lacerate my neck and arm, drawing more blood. It repels them like smoke repels gnats. The more I bleed, the wider my path grows. I am rushing through, giddy with pain and excitement.

Until I run smack into a glassy wall.

I blink, trying to reconcile the smoothness of the obstacle with the tangle of twigs and branches.

My questing fingers explore it, my eyes are straining, trying to make out anything in the crawling infestation of shadows. The star is still above me, shedding her cool unflinching light, but the thorn trees have grown so thick that I can barely make out anything. It's a wall—this is certain. And a very high wall. I cannot see where it ends. And a smooth wall, so smooth that my fingers keep sliding off it.

I lean closer, peer into the wall. It has depth, and this depth is swarming with silver motes like a frozen pond swarming with tiny fish. But it is not ice. Ice on a warm spring night would be a miracle. This is something far more miraculous.

It is the sky.

I have reached the boundary where the dome of the sky touches the floor of our valley. No surprise I cannot see where the wall ends because it does not. It covers the valley under its smooth sweep the star fixed at its highest point. The sky that Udmur and Umar have placed above us, trapping us under it like an insect trapped under an overturned glass.

For a long time, I am lost in the wonder and excitement of it, but then a disquieting thought occurs to me. As I was running through the Thorny Wood, I heard a distant cock's crow. Morning is coming, the globe of the sun would roll up the dome of the sky, coming from beneath the floor of the valley. The sun always rises at the same spot over the Thorny Wood, and this spot is close to where I am now. The sun is hot; I have been burned often enough working in the fields to know that. What will happen to me if it passes too close? Won't I be incinerated by its radiance?

I turn around to run back through the woods to the safety of our farm and gasp. The trees repelled by my blood have come back together, twined, and twisted closer than before. Behind me, a tall barricade bristles with knife-sharp barbs. I unlocked it before with my own blood, but the wall seems denser now. Is there enough blood in my veins to open this passage?

The sky-wall in front of me is brightening. No longer is the cold radiance of the star the only light in my world. The glassy surface is washed with peach and rose, the tender colors of dawn climbing up to the zenith. But with light comes heat. The wall is warming, each new spurt of color and light bringing an exhalation of warm air. At first it feels good, but it takes only a couple of heartbeats for the heat to grow from pleasant to scorching. My face is beaded with sweat. My breath comes in short gasps. My eyes are drying out. The thorns behind me inch closer, and the fiery edge of the sun is peeking from under my feet, through the tangle of roots.

Desperate, I hammer on the sky-wall with the sword-shard and then with my bare hands, leaving slicks of blood.

The wall opens up. A small section of it swings out. Behind it, I can see nothing but swirls of clotted mist. I do not care. Anything is preferable to death by fire.

I drop to my knees and squeeze through the narrow opening. When my feet are out, the door swings shut with an audible clank and I am left clinging to a rough surface that feels like tree bark, gasping and shivering.

What is it? Where am I?

Gradually I unglue myself from my perch, stand up, and look around. The immensity of this space takes my breath away. I never imagined that there can be so much emptiness in the world. Where is the sky? Where is the ground? Where is the star or the sun? All around me is a misty void, lilac and mauve and pale blue, thickening into twilight, and never-ending, drawing my gaze on and on until I feel I am running away from myself. And this twilight infinity is crisscrossed with dark angled lines, like strokes of writing on colored paper. It makes no sense until suddenly it flips and resolves itself into something familiar.

The lines are boughs.

Yes, tree boughs. How can it be? Even the limbs of the trees in the Thorny Wood are not sturdy enough to bear the weight of a grown woman. But here I am, and I am not clinging to the bough anymore. I am standing on it. I am an ant, a tiny insect, and the branch is as wide as the road that leads from my parents' farm to the heart of the valley. I can walk on it, and I do.

Have I shrunk? No sooner does this thought occur to me as my vision contradicts it. The branch is narrower than it looks. Or maybe wider? It expands and contracts as if the giant tree were breathing, but with no regularity. It flickers in and out of perspective.

Size means nothing here. As I am walking along the branch, it unrolls into a broad highway and then suddenly dwindles so much that I need to drop down on my hands and knees in order not to fall into the void. Still, if I disregard these distortions, I can make out the general shape of this...place? Or is it space?

The tree looms above me, disappearing into the misty expanse. Below me, it plunges into the abyss. No sky above, no ground below. The branch I am on is growing from the stupendous craggy trunk. Radiating from the trunk are other boughs, bare and devoid of twigs or secondary branches. But not devoid of fruit. Drooping off them are rounded glossy balls, attached to the boughs by long shiny tendrils or stalks. Where the stalk enters the ball, there is a silvery coupling like that of an acorn.

There is no sun. No star. No sky. Just this fluid immensity all around me, and I feel like my mind and body are swelling, expanding, filling with lightness, and floating away from me. I am a balloon. I am a mote. I am everything and nothing. I walk along the bark highway that is as wide as our valley, and I cling to a fragile twig that I can snap with my fingers. The tree is the universe. The tree is just a tree.

I come to a fork and I decide to rest. I sit down, my legs dangling over the abyss, and squint as I look back, trying to gauge where I came out. Then I see movement. Something is approaching. A dark shape is running, leaping, zigzagging toward me. Another escapee from the prison of the valley?

But as the shape gets closer, I realize it is not a human being. It is four-legged, shaggy, and black— an ugly blot on the softly shining mist. It is swelling, growing bigger with every leap it takes.

Tanri!

I recognize him though I have never seen him. A wolfdog, a wooly tangle of limbs, a slavering maw, and a pair of red eyes. He is shifting like a blot of ink dripped into water, changing shape and dimensions, sometimes looming as tall as a farmhouse, sometimes shrinking to the size of a sheepdog. But no matter how big or how small, I know he is dangerous. And that he hates me. I feel this hate coming off him in waves of hot stinking breath, tinged with the stench of old rotting blood.

"Yildiz," a sibilant voice says behind me.

I turn. Coiling around the trunk is a huge serpent. His body is milky-white and glittering with pinpricks of light. His eyes are large and blue—

human eyes, fringed with long, sensuous lashes. His forked tongue is the color of a rose petal.

"Udmur and Umar defend me!" I shout a childhood prayer,

"Udmur and Umar are dead," the serpent responds.

"And who are you?"

"Mor."

The name means nothing to me, and my gaze shifts away from the serpent to the bounding form of Tanri. He is shrinking as he approaches me, but that only makes him more frightening. A wolf the size of a mountain will shake me off like a louse; a wolf the size of a dog will tear me to pieces.

"My brother has gone crazy," the serpent notes conversationally. "He does not like the ripening world-fruit. You'd better be careful, Yildiz. He can swallow you whole."

"Your brother?"

"We are both children of Oyun, but he is dead, too. Nobody left but Tanri and me."

"Can you stop him?"

"He won't listen to me."

"Thanks for nothing!" I snarl.

My fear has not dissipated, but somehow it has refined itself into rage. I lift my broken sword and take a fighting position, one that I saw Safet practice with his father. The serpent hisses, and I realize he is laughing. Tanri's maw gapes wide, foamy saliva dripping off his fangs, his rotting-blood breath hitting me full in the face.

I stand no chance! A small slender girl against a huge monster...

And as I think this, I feel myself start to grow. It feels as natural as stretching after a long nap. My muscles unfold like flower petals. My bones lengthen painlessly. My hair flows down my shoulders in a trickle of darkness like a river, a waterfall.

My fingers curl around the sword shard, and it disappears into the folds of my skin. The bough I am standing on expands in swirls of wood and bark to bear my growing weight. I am the size of a farmhouse. I am the size of the valley. I am the size of the universe.

I pick up a fluff of black hair at my feet. It is twitching and shuddering, and though its growl is almost too high-pitched to hear, I can sense its frenzy. I blow on it. The fluff sails off my palm and disappears into the twilight.

"Well done," a hissing voice says behind my back.

I turn around. The serpent has grown to match my size. Coiling around the trunk of the World-Tree, he is regarding me with sly blue eyes.

"No thanks to you," I say churlishly.

"What are you complaining about? The gods are dead. The Last War, Savas, has come and gone. And here we are, playing in the aftermath, while the world-fruit is ripening on Zivana, the Tree of Trees."

"World-fruit?"

"Each of them is a world. If planted, it may expand into a universe."

And then I understand. I reach out and cup one of the satiny spheres. It is small enough—or rather, I am large enough—that it can fit snugly into my palm. It is slick and warm. The silvery cupule connects the fruit to the stalk which grows into it. I know that where the stalk enters the sphere, a fixed silver nail shines in the glassy sky.

"A good choice!" the serpent says.

Lying in my hand is my world. The valley, the Thorny Wood, the sun, and the star. The farmhouse where I was born and where my sister Hayat is waking up in her cot, my mother smiling at her as she has never smiled to me. With one twitch of my fingers, I can crush it all.

"You can smash it, if you want," the serpent says leisurely. "There are many other worlds out there. See, they are all hanging on the tree, ready to be plucked. Planted or discarded, it's all up to us. We are the only ones left."

"Am I a goddess?"

Again, his mocking laughter. "There are no gods anymore. No rules. We can make our own."

I can make a world in which fratricide is a virtue. I can make a world in which I am the sole divinity. I can make a world in which my parents are burning forever in the fires of the eternal sun.

Little snippets of memories flash before my eyes. I remember Hayat, gurgling in her cot, her toothless mouth smiling at me. I remember my mother wiping my forehead with a cool cloth as I burned with fever. I remember long lazy afternoons spend with Safet in the orchard, and the tartness of the apples he plucked for me.

I relax my hand, and the valley of my birth swings gently on its stalk, as my parents look up in fear and hope to the silver star suddenly moving in the sky.

"What happens when a world-fruit is planted?" I ask the serpent.

"It grows, sprouting valleys and mountains, rivers and seas. Places to settle in, places to avoid."

"No more walls?"

"No more walls."

"I think this one is ready to plant," I say.

The Tale of Lady Evangeline
by K.A. Kenny

It was colder than she'd expected, one of those March nights when winter regains its sway, and Lady Evangeline feared she might be lost. Her handmaidens had told her how to find the old wise woman—known in whispered circles for helping troubled women. But alone in the dark wood, Evangeline despaired of ever finding the rustic cottage.

A gusting wind lashed bare branches over the face of the moon and shifted long shadows on the forest floor. Evangeline pulled her thin scarf close around her head and tucked a wave of raven hair back from her eyes. When she looked up again there the cottage stood, crafted in the trunk of a gnarled tree.

Ridges of moonlight and darkness gave the cottage the appearance of a troll's face—the twisted doorway, a disfigured mouth; two misaligned windows, the squinting, wrinkled eyes; and the broken stump of a branch for a nose.

The sight gave Lady Evangeline a start and filled her with foreboding. Lifting her white linen gown clear of the mud and turning to leave, she caught her foot on a knotted tree root that seemed to reach up like a back-broken snake.

"Milady," called a frail, high-pitched voice. One of the squinting cottage eyes glinted as a candle was lit. "Have you come to pay an old woman a visit? Please come in."

The bent figure that came to the doorway grinned a broken, four-toothed smile. Her balding, brown-splotched pate reminded Evangeline of the skull Father Joska kept on his scribing desk. The crone beseeched her so earnestly to come that Evangeline felt too ashamed to refuse. So, lifting her gown high in her long white hands to clear the roots, she followed the woman inside.

The musty, one-room cottage had an ash-filled stone hearth with glowing embers, a slatted bed with a deerskin blanket, and a rough-hewn wooden table with two rickety chairs. Peg-mounted shelves above the table held ceramic jars, glass bottles and flasks, and dust-covered books. A straw broom stood in one corner and earthen flagons in the others. The only light came from the full moon in the window, candles on the table and windowsills, and hearth embers.

The woman shooed a black cat from one of the chairs. The cat hissed and clawed, leaping away only when threatened with a broom. "Fester hasn't seen many high-born ladies," she explained, offering the chair to Evangeline. Though her words were pleasant, the old woman's cracked voice and the curve of her thin smile sent chills up Evangeline's back.

"I am Matta Crowley," said the crone, lifting a kettle from the hearth.

"I know," Evangeline said firmly.

"Some toadwort tea?" When Evangeline's thin brows shot up, the woman added, "Toadwort is native to this forest, it makes a fine herbal tea." Evangeline nodded, and Matta Crowley filled two brown-stained, wooden cups.

"How nice you are to visit me. I was told you might come by. Tell me, my Lady, what might an old woman do for a beautiful young princess?"

"My handmaidens said you might be able to help me. I—"

Evangeline suddenly burst into tears. She covered her eyes with a white, lace-trimmed kerchief clutched in her delicate, milk-white hands. When she tried to continue, her words broke into sobs, shakes, and sniffing.

"A broken heart is it?" Tiny curls crept into the corners of a slit-like, lipless mouth.

Evangeline nodded, dropping her gaze and her folded hands to her lap. After two long breaths, she pulled erect. "I think I shall never love again. Never. I'm only sixteen, and this has never happened to me." She pushed her long hair behind a shoulder with a trembling hand.

Matta Crowley slid one eye to Evangeline's untouched teacup then sipped from her own. "Warm tea will help you feel better, dear child," said the high, cracking voice.

Evangeline buried her face in her quivering hands, sobbing tears flowing freely. The crone touched a jagged, yellow claw to Evangeline's arm and stroked her black, flowing hair. "Now, now, my dear, I know it hurts. Tell me what favor you wish from me?"

"I want to never feel this pain again. I hurt so much, so very, very much. And I know..."

Evangeline stopped to swallow. "I know it will never ever end."

"There, there, my sweet one. Sixteen is a very tender age, and there is much I can do with you. But are you sure this is what you want, for your pain to go away? Here, my child, drink some tea." She nudged the teacup closer.

Evangeline picked it up, but, seeing her hands moist with tears, returned it to the table and touched the lace-trimmed kerchief to her hands, fingers, and eyes. When she finally reached for the cup and drank, a smiled widened on Matta Crowley's face.

"Can you truly take my pain away?" Evangeline asked, her delicate hands twisting her kerchief.

The old woman's eyes glowed like coals in their dark, hollow sockets. "Is it just the pain you want removed or the memory also? Or perhaps something more?" Her thin mouth drew into a gap-toothed sneer.

Evangeline took a gasping breath. "I...I must keep the memory, so...so I remember never do this again. But, yes, oh yes, I want the pain to go away." She brushed a tear from her downcast cheek then returned her hand to her lap. "This morning Sir Reginald told me he had to return to his betrothed in Andalusia. His betrothed? How...how could he do this? All summer he told me he loved me. He said I was the only one." She stared beyond the crone now, and her mouth tightened. "I had many suitors. Many handsome men wanted me. But I chose Sir Reginald...and he ruined me. He asked me for my favors, and I granted them, favors I promised my mother I would never give to anyone until I married—"

"Yes, dear child, I understand. I was young once and beautiful, and men loved and desired me." She sighed and closed her eyes wistfully then laughed. "But I made the mistake of loving one back."

Evangeline tried to imagine the sunken, dung-colored figure as a young woman.

Matta Crowley continued. "I was given the choice to be loved and to enjoy that love but never to love in return."

Evangeline's eyes took on a new glow. "Oh, that is a choice I would willingly make. What must I do?"

The old woman lifted a small black bottle from the shelf above. Cradling the bottle in her clawed fingers, she removed the stopper.

"One drop upon your tongue will make you eternally young and beautiful to all desirable men, and you will forget the pain of having ever loved." A crooked smile tightened across her broken teeth.

"Eternally young and beautiful?" Evangeline squinched her face in disbelief.

"Only to desirable young men," Crowley said. "Others will see you as you truly are. Every young man who gazes upon you will burn for you. Having once seen you, he will give his heart instantly and completely. He will want you and no other, and having given his heart, he will be incapable of ever loving another."

"And I will feel nothing?"

"You will feel as he does, but only for a single night, and only with your loins and your lips—never with your heart, for there is where the pain lies. You will share his flaming passion, but come morning, he will only disgust you. And that disgust will take away all your pain."

"But can I never love again...truly love?"

"Dear child, have you not tasted true love? You said you never wanted it again."

Evangeline pressed her delicate, white hands to her face and nodded. "Yes, the cost is too high."

"My Lady," a deep voice boomed. "Excuse me, my beloved, I see you are busy, perhaps another time."

Evangeline was startled to see her father's knight standing in the dark doorway, his hands clasped before his sky-blue tunic as if in prayer. Sir Geoffrey had pursued her last year, but she had already chosen Reginald. How had he followed her...and on such a night? How dare he after she'd rejected him, and after she'd caught him in her handmaid's chamber.

Before Evangeline could protest, Geoffrey rushed past her to kneel at the foot of the old crone. "My Lady, you are the fairest, most desirable woman I have ever known." Evangeline stared in utter confusion. "Please let me hear one kind word from your lips. My dearest one, I curse myself for whatever I did to lose your favor."

Matta Crowley rested her ragged hand on the knight's bowed head and stroked his dark, candle-lit curls. "If you wish to please me, Sir Geoffrey, some venison would be welcome or a wild pig for the roasting spit. Would you do that for your beloved?"

"I will hunt for you, fair lady. And when I return, I will prepare the meat for you." With that, he left without giving Evangeline a second glance.

The old woman laced her clawed fingers above the table and peered over them. "You see how the magic works, dear child. If you visit your Sir Reginald once again, his passion will ignite more fiercely than ever. You may enjoy him as you wish, then be rid of him. As your passion cools to contempt, his will grow to eternal torment."

"And he will feel what he made me feel." Evangeline huffed a laugh, rested her chin on her raised, delicately folded hands, and looked across at Matta Crowley. "My handmaidens said you were a witch, but I didn't believe them."

The old woman lifted the kettle to offer the lady more tea. "Yes, I am a witch, and so shall you be, my child. So, shall you be."

THE END

A Murky Mess

by Benjamin Zahm

Hildwulf stared into the crackling orange glow of a small fire before him. A thin wisp of grey smoke rose lazily from the small pile of twigs, causing the hordes of mosquitos patrolling the humid air to pull back in disgust.

Looking up from the blaze, Hildwulf once again scanned the dismal marsh around him. Putrid water laced with green algae surrounded the small rise of ground he'd sought refuge on. In all directions, similar patches of boggy earth rose from the swamp-like a bale of ghostly turtles, and every few yards, a gnarled tree jutted unevenly from the sludge. A light green fog covered everything and accompanied a heavy, rotten smell that seemed appropriate for the dreary wasteland. The air was filled with the croaking and creaking of countless frogs and crickets populating the bleak landscape, and every so often, a small bird would swoosh between the trees.

Hildwulf had been in the swamp for over three weeks, and his food supply was nearly exhausted. He'd dug up some roots, eaten the few berries that grew, and shot several of the small birds to extend his stay. Unfortunately, the meat had a gritty, vile taste, and he quickly gave up hunting the little scavengers.

Hildwulf tossed another twig on the merry orange glow, then turned his attention to the papyrus laid out beside him. Selecting a sharpened piece of black charcoal, he drew several marks on the coarse document. Some said this marsh was impermeable. Others said it was bewitched and that only the gods themselves would dare try to inhabit its rancid terrain. Hildwulf, on the other hand, smiled in satisfaction at nature's display of unchecked might. Here was a living abyss that could withstand years of man's efforts to convert it into narrow streets and cold grey buildings.

Nature regulated itself to a perfect utopia. The strong preyed on the weak. The weak on the helpless. However, it was only a matter of time before the strong succumbed to their own predators. The weak would grow from feeding on the remains of their hunters, at least until another came along.

Everything went full circle, keeping everything as it should be.

Hildwulf hadn't always believed such things. He had recently been re-educated by a band of woodland clerics who had nursed him back to health shortly after being badly injured.

He'd thought that fight—one spurred on by rousing speeches and a dazzling call to arms—had had been the *right fight*. . It had felt like he was a part of something. Something bigger than life. Sadly, that fulfillment was short-lived. The righteous battlefield which was promised never came. Instead, Hildwulf found himself participating in cowardly raids, often catching unsuspecting villages in the carnage.

Thinking of it now caused Hildwulf's stomach to churn in disgust. There had been nothing worth fighting for there. The castle lords cared not for the damage their cohorts inflicted on the people land or their own troops if it furthered their own means. Hildwulf's wound, however life-threatening, had only served as a symbol of the turmoil within. Now he chose his conflicts. Never again would he allow another to drag him into a fight that wasn't his.

Although Hildwulf had learned a great deal, he was never blessed with the cleric's divine divination. Perhaps he was impatient, or maybe he had simply gone too far in his past life to ever make it back. He found what salvation he could in nature, living as a ranger, away from humanity's mad scramble for power.

A sudden, unexpected sound drew Hildwulf back to the present moment.

"Dedu, stop splashing!" a squeaky voice said in the distance.

Quickly rolling his half-finished outline of the swamp, Hildwulf stuffed it inside a waterproof cylinder. Then he grabbed his bow and loosely set an arrow on the string.

"I not splashing. You splashing!"

The voice drew nearer, and Hildwulf distinguished the sound of several feet sloshing through the muck. In another moment, three small goblins, garbed in grey strips of cloth, emerged from a thicket of reeds. Two goblins carried short spears, while a machete was nonchalantly slung over the shoulder of the third. Hildwulf had instinctively dropped out of sight, but the goblins' keen eyes quickly spotted him, and with a gleeful shriek, they splashed over to him. Hildwulf wasn't sure what to do, so he simply stood to his feet and held his bow ready at his side.

"What yor name?" the goblin carrying the machete asked as he squatted next to Hildwulfs small fire. "Whatcha doing onna wimbat land?"

"My name is Hildwulf," the ranger answered warily. "I'm just passing through." He eyed the trio of goblins clustered around his small fire.

"Whats inna bag?" the goblin holding the machete asked as he jabbed his weapon toward Hildwulf's brown leather pouch lying on the ground.

"That's none of your concern." Hildwulf gripped his bow tighter.

The goblin frowned, pouting his lips as he eyed Hildwulf. "I aska real nice what inna bag?"

Hildwulf shifted slightly. "Just a few supplies."

The goblin stood and scanned Hildwulf from head to foot, much like a spoiled six-year-old. "Nice shiny bladez. Gimme doze," He pointed to the knife and sword on Hildwulfs belt.

Hildwulf shook his head. "I'm afraid not."

The goblin seemed annoyed at his refusal, and his lips pouted fiercely as he did a small dance of fury. "You onna wimbat land. Big chief say you havva pay tribute."

"Big chief nevva say dat," one of the other goblins said, scratching his head.

This perturbed the first goblin even more, and he stamped his foot in indignation. "Shuddup, Tazz! Alway pay tribute starta now!" He whirled to face Hildwulf and drew a finger across his throat. "Uddawise you go bye-bye."

"Dedu, what you doing onna neck?" the one called Tazz asked in puzzlement.

The third goblin leaned in close to the second, a look of grave concern on his face. "I think Dedu gotta itchy onna neck."

At this, the two of them burst into cackling laughter and fell back on the wet piece of land.

"No, you fooz notta itchy onna neck," Dedu squeaked angrily, clutching his fists. "Dis mean I kill him."

"Dedu canna kill big man," the third goblin laughed, wiping a tear away from his eye. "Das, why big chief kicked us outta tribe."

Dedu valiantly puffed out his little chest and held his machete high in the air. "If we kill dis guy and take his goodies, then big chief will know we big an' strong. Then we kin go home again!"

The two other goblins went silent as Hildwulf rose to his full height.

Dedu seemed to realize he'd lost his companion's support, and he hung his head in shame. "Dedu, sorry."

Hildwulf replaced the arrow in his quiver. Strangely he felt no anger at the goblins' blatant intent to kill him. If anything, he almost felt sorry. These goblins, however ill their intent, just wanted a ticket home.

"Pick your fights and make sure they're ones you can win," Hildwulf said, offering the only advice he knew.

"I...keep tying." Dedu sighed, seeming to study the mud squeezed between his toes.

He glanced up at Hildwulf sheepishly. Hildwulf just nodded, and the trio of goblins retreated from the now nearly extinguished fire. Hildwulf watched carefully as the creatures sloshed wordlessly away, and he couldn't help but shake his head in amazement.

"Funny little things." He said with a forced chuckle. Tossing several small branches on the fire, he tried to settle back in.

"Deeeeeduuuuuuuu!" A high, piercing cry split the swamp's muffled atmosphere, and Hildwulf started in surprise. Gripping his bow, he stared in the direction the goblins had gone.

"Ahhhhh. Lemme go! Lemme go!" A high voice, unmistakably Dedu's, squealed in protest.

There was a loud splash, and Dedu's two companions added their cries to the ruckus. "Naughty! Drop him! Drop him right now!"

Hildwulf thought the noise might be a trap to lure him forward, but the cries were so convincing that he found himself quickly nocking another arrow and plunging ahead anyway.

The murky water rose midway up Hildwulf's thighs, and thick mud clung to his boots as he plowed forward. Behind him, a trail lay broken through the layers of green algae. Water spiders scuttled frantically to get out of his way. Climbing up onto another rise of earth, Hildwulf surveyed the scene before him. A giant, wrinkled troll stood just ahead. Held tightly in one of its hands was the sputtering Dedu. At his side, the goblin's two companions were jabbing their little spears fiercely at the troll's calves. The beast did not seem to notice.

"Die, die, die, you big ol' toad!"

The two goblins continued to poke their spears at one of the troll's leathery legs. The dull creature finally realized and glanced down at the two imps. With a swift kick, the troll sent the two goblins sailing through the air. They disappeared into the dark water with a splash.

Dedu still gripped his machete, and this he swung wildly in the air as the troll lifted him upside down. "Yargh! Eat dis, you big fattie!"

Realizing the troll was about to rip the little idiot in half, Hildwulf drew his bow and leveled it toward the hulking creature. He paused. *"Nature takes care of its own,"* Hildwulf remembered the cleric's words.

This goblin was nothing but a dot in a world of giants. There had been hundreds of thousands like him, and there would undoubtedly be millions more. Nature conducted and regulated itself regardless of the participants. Or did it?

True nature often pitted unfair combatants against one another, but that didn't mean Hildwulf was somehow separate or above it all. He was a part of nature that could adapt to or influence those around him. Nature allowed him to make decisions, and he was free to stay or turn around and leave. No castle lord holed up behind stone walls was dictating his every move. This was his choice and his alone.

Straightening his bow, which had lowered Hildwulf, he drew back. Paused for a split second. Then released.

This would be his fight because he made it his fight.

The arrow sank into the back of the troll's gnarled hand with a bone–crunching zip. The troll's thick, knotted fingers spasmed, and Dedu fell headlong into the water below.

The troll roared angrily, its head instantly swiveling in Hildwulf's direction Hildwulf quickly moved to nock another arrow on the string, but before he had a chance to loose it, the troll was upon him. Hildwulf rolled to his left as the troll crashed a fist down where he'd just been standing. Quickly recovering to one knee, he loosed his arrow into the troll's side. Instead of howling in pain, the brute responded with a heavy backhand. The impact stunned Hildwulf, who suddenly found himself flying through the air before landing in the dank water with a resounding splash.

Under the water, everything was dark and muffled. Particles of black and brown algae swirled around him. The light from above barely pierced the surface. Choking on the foul liquid, Hildwulf painfully sat up, the water swirling around his neck and shoulders. The troll's punch had knocked the air out of him, and his lungs refused to open.

"What you tryna do, drown Dedu?" Beside Hildwulf, the small goblin sputtered wildly in the putrid water.

Hildwulf's hearing was fuzzy, but somehow the little brat's high voice cut straight through the fog in his head. "A simple thank you will suffice," Hildwulf wheezed.

The troll was lumbering toward him. A long, gnarled branch clutched in one hand.

"I notta say dank you, you makka big fattie mad!" Dedu rushed to stand behind the bigger man.

Hildwulf's lungs released, and he drew a shaky breath. Drawing an arrow from his quiver, Hildwulf stood to his feet and raised his bow from the water. The entire upper shaft of his bow had snapped clean in half, leaving two pieces of curved wood tied together with a thin string.

"No, not good!" Hildwulf clenched his jaw.

"You's in big trouble now," Dedu said quietly as the troll stepped within striking distance.

Hildwulf threw himself to the right as the troll swung its branch in a powerful downward arch that slapped the water with a horrific noise. Quickly hauling himself back onto his feet, Hildwulf drew his sword and whirled to face the brute. Hildwulf considered drawing his knife but opted to use both hands for his sword, which offered him more reach.

"Dedu?" he called, wondering if the troll's blow had hit the little imp.

"Whatcha want?" Hildwulf looked down and found Dedu standing beside him.

'Where did you come from?"

"Helping Tazz an Bleel a course," Dedu replied, motioning backward. Hildwulf wanted to look, but the troll had again drawn within striking distance, forcing him to retreat. Suddenly Hildwulf stumbled. Something beneath the water, undoubtedly a fallen tree, had snagged his boot. Half-falling, half-swimming, Hildwulf floundered in muddy water. The troll seeing Hidwulf's struggle, eagerly sprang forward, weapon raised. But without warning, the troll also tripped. Hildwulf felt the tree limbs beneath the water lurch forward from the troll's impact, and he instantly yanked his boot free. Just as he did, the troll's upper body hit the water, sending a wave of water crashing over him. Still half-swimming, Hildwulf clumsily pulled away from the mess before quickly wiping the water from his eyes.

Several paces to his left, Dedu stood wide-eyed.

"Listen, Dedu," Hildwulf spoke hurriedly. "I want you to run back to my camp and grab a fiery branch. You got it?"

"Gonna burn da big, nasty monsta?" Dedu asked, breaking from his stupor.

"Yeah, something like that, now go!" Hildwulf ordered, his breathing ragged. Dedu hesitated, then turned and took off running toward Hildwulf's camp.

"And now for you," Hildwulf said, turning his attention back to his towering opponent. The troll had already untangled itself from the web of waterlogged limbs and quickly lurched forward. It swung its sword-like branch in a blur, leaving Hildwulf only milliseconds to react. Ducking under the blow, Hildwulf sprang forward and slashed his weapon across the troll's upper thigh. The brute immediately kicked its leg forward, attempting to crush him. With a quick bound, Hildwulf dodged the attack and once again sliced his sword across the troll's unprotected leg.

The troll was furious at this and swung its weapon in a full circle just above the surface of the water, leaving Hildwulf nowhere to flee but down. He submerged himself in the murky water. Just above, the tree branch swished over the water, causing a knot to form in Hildwulf's stomach.

As soon as the weapon passed, Hildwulf emerged from the water to re-engage. Only this time, the troll was ready for him. As Hildwulf sprang up, the beast's massive leathery foot came crashing down. All Hildwulf could do was take a quick gasp of air before he was pushed back under the surface of the water. Muck swirled all around as he was slammed into the bottom of the bog. His one gasp of air nearly exploded from his mouth. The troll's foot ground him further into the mire, and Hildwulf felt one of his ribs pop under the tremendous pressure.

Pure panic set in. Bubbles exploded from Hidwulf's mouth as he frantically dropped his sword and jabbed his knife into the troll's foot. The brute bellowed in anguish. It yanked its foot off his chest as plumes of blood clouded the water. Hildwulf rose, gasping for breath, sharp pain in his chest. His ears rung, and he felt like vomiting the wretched water he'd accidentally inhaled.

"Here we is!"

Hildwulf retreated several steps, then glanced to his left. Dedu and his two companions were wading toward him. Clutched in Dedu's hand was a brightly burning branch. Across his face was a devilish grin.

"We bringed fire jus like you wanted, an we gotted it real—"

Dedu's words were cut short. His bright smile disappeared under the water as he tripped and fell headlong into the muck. The flaming branch followed and extinguished with a loud hiss.

Hildwulf felt his heart sink, but he had no time to waste. The troll had already recovered. With a roar, it sprang toward him. Still, dizzy, Hildwulf weakly dodged to the right, gripping his knife with white knuckles. It was the only weapon he had left now. The troll seemed to be adapting to Hildwulf's methods, and, clumsily sidestepping, it caught him with a sweeping blow that sent the man tumbling through the air again. But this time, he landed on one of the murky islands.

The hard landing stunned his already dazed body. Above him, Hildwulf heard a faint crackling and, opening his eyes, saw Tazz standing over him with a blazing torch.

"Want da fire?" the goblin asked, holding the light closer to Hildwulf's head.

"Y-yes." Hildwulf gasped, seizing the flame and rolling painfully onto his knees.

Looking up, the ranger saw Dedu and Bleel flinging rocks and other objects at the troll, slowing the brute's advance upon Hildwulf's position. Digging through the soggy pouch slung over his shoulder, Hildwulf withdrew a round flask. Stepping forward, he hurled the container at the troll's massive head. The bottle broke apart. A shiny oil quickly covered the brute's body.

"Hey, you two, watch out!" Hildwulf yelled as he stepped forward.

He flung his crackling torch upon the stunned monster. The oil caught the blazing flame, and in an instant, the troll was engulfed in sheets of angry, red fire. The beast wailed in agony. It thrashed wildly at the flames. However, the fire could not be so easily defeated. The troll staggered blindly before collapsing onto its knees, still tearing at the surrounding inferno.

Seeing his chance, Hildwulf seized a short spear from the goblin beside him and lept forward. The heat from the blaze was terrifying, but the ranger endured, advancing directly in front of the towering beast. With a mighty thrust, he ended the threat for good.

The troll toppled over without a sound, its body sizzling as it entered the cold water. Clouds of white steam bubbled up into the air. Hildwulf kept a firm grip on the weapon for a moment longer, then satisfied the beast was dead, he fell back onto the wet ground.

"Did Hidwof kill da big naughty monsta?" Dedu asked, cautiously approaching.

Hildwulf was too tired to reply.

"Is a big baddie," Dedu said, angrily kicking the troll's submerged carcass then pulling his foot back in anguish.

"Is a big ol monsta, sure nuff. Yous did mighty good, Hodwoof!" Bleel said, eyeing the ranger appreciatively.

"What we do now?" Tazz asked.

"I sure would like my sword back, but I suppose it's long gone." Hildwulf groaned, scanning the mere around them.

"Psht," Dedu said. "Not fo me! Nothing long gone fo Dedu." And so, saying, Dedu dragged Hildwulf's sword from the water.

"Dedu, you marvelous little freak. Thank you!" Hildwulf lifted Dedu and spun him round and round.

"Whooh, oh no. Dedu not wanna be sicked. Leave Dedu alone!"

Hildwulf continued his spin for a moment longer, then dropped the squirming goblin. Then he gratefully returned his sword to its scabbard.

"What now?" Dedu asked.

Hildwulf smiled through aches and bruises. "I keep mapping out the swamp, and you three return to your tribe to tell your big chief about the huge monster you've slain."

The trio of goblins seemed confused for a moment, then Dedu's eyes widened in understanding.

"Oooh, oh, hahaha, I gets it! I get's it!" He laughed uncontrollably. "Dedu an' his two pals da big monsta slaying heroes." He chuckled even more as he and his companions turned and began trudging off. But before they'd gone more than a few feet, Dedu paused and spun around to face Hildwulf.

"I glad you keeped the bladez." He smiled. "Too big fo Dedu anyway."

Hildwulf smiled back. "For now."

Dedu opened his mouth to say something, but for once, nothing came out. "You's much good," he finally managed. Then they turned and sloshed away.

Hildwulf's brow furrowed in confusion. *"Yous much good?"* Suddenly he understood. The goblin language had no proper word for thanks, so Dedu had done the best he could to show gratitude. The goblins had all but disappeared into the swamp, but through the trees, Hildwulf could hear Dedu narrating the story of their fight.

"An' den I poked him inna eye an' said, 'how's you like dat you big fattie?'"

"An' I was jabbing my spear inna his bum until couldn't sit down ebber again!" Tazz said with a laugh.

"An once he falled down, I jumped up an' down onna his head an' said 'you nebber gon get rid of dis headache you nasty ol toad!'" Bleel added.

Hildwulf laughed as he listened to the goblin's voices slowly fade into the distance. Dedu and his companions were mere dots on the grand scale of things, but then again, so was Hildwulf. And it was true the strong preyed on the weak, but that did not make it right, nor did it mean the weak had no right to live. Hildwulf's head swam as he suddenly remembered something his father had taught him, the lesson that had started him on the warrior's path.

"Any fool can stand up for themselves. One with heart will stand up for others."

THE END

Queen of the Shrydland

by James W. Barnes

Nothing good will come from this meeting." The former king held his daughter's steel eyes with his own firm glare. His short white beard framed a resolute jaw. "I will prevent it."

Maab knew he could, but her own determination met his with equal strength.

"You are my father," she said. "Not my advisor." She rose carefully from her satin cloaked throne and stepped toward the arched stone window overlooking the castle gardens below. "It is too late, Father. I have summoned him in my capacity as queen of the Shrydland."

"Summoned him?" Her father strode to her. "You dare to invite this dark magician into our midst when you know he is a death-eater?"

She looked him in the eyes. "Yes! And may he well eat the death that has stolen my husband from me!" She put her hand to her full stomach. "As I carry our child, death dares to take his father from us, and before him, my mother? I will find any means to speak to my husband from beyond the grave. My most powerful ally in this endeavor is Armenthraal, the one you call a death-eater."

She gathered her robe, knowing the autumn evening would be chilled. She hoped her personal warriors at the gate had received her orders and would be waiting there for her, and that the vicious Followers were crouching ready at the forest edge. She paused at the corridor entrance and remembered how she and her father had been so close in earlier years, and how much she missed having the loving presence of her mother. Since the former queen's death, her father had turned cold to her, somehow suspecting she was responsible. Perhaps she was. Perhaps her mother could not accept a daughter's strange fascination with dark magic.

"I will prevent this, Maab," her father said softly. "You know I have the means even in my abdicated choice. I cannot allow you to bring this poison into the Shrydland, not when ravaging beasts roam our forest and have killed both your mother and your husband."

"It was not meant to happen!" she cried out, freezing in the doorway. "They misunderstood my command," she said softly, more to herself.

"What did you say?" her father asked, stepping cautiously toward her.

"I said my command to them was misheard." She inhaled deeply, unsure she should reveal her secret. "I have them under my control."

Her father stared at her in what Maab interpreted as grief mixed with horror. "You play with these beasts that killed your mother and husband? You—you control them? Have I lost the daughter I once held and sang heroic ballads to by the river? Who are you now since this insatiable fascination with death-magic has become your constant obsession? Where have you hidden my daughter whom I love?"

He stood so dumfounded that Maab decided she would no longer respond to his questions. She felt a hint of tears struggling to break free. She did not allow them. She glanced into her father's wide eyes as she brushed past him and made her heavy but still elegant way to the stairs that led to the castle entrance. She heard him calling after her and then to his private guard. His voice was more desperate than she had ever known it.

Maab met her loyal warriors at the door. Both were prepared for battle. The lead warrior raised his arm and soon seven others appeared beside them.

"We must hurry! My father will pursue us!"

"Yes, Queen Maab," the lead warrior assented as he and another helped lift her onto the horse they held for her. "But surely your father's guard will be strong, my Queen."

"Of course they will, Morleck. But you will be stronger." The armored warrior nodded and signaled to the others who mounted and rode as swiftly as their pregnant queen could allow them toward the tree-lined river beneath the castle hill. Maab could hear her father's guards' pursuit. She hoped they would choose not to engage their queen in battle, but she knew her father still wielded enough authority to convince them to do so.

When they reached the river's edge, she saw a red swirling haze a short distance upstream. The summer sun had sunk behind the tall willows lining the riverbanks, highlighting the glowing hue.

"It's the necromancer!" she shouted aloud.

But as her warriors helped her from her saddle the king's loyal guards arrived, swords drawn. There were twenty of them to her nine.

"My Lady, your father, king of the Shrydland, has given us orders to bring you back to the castle with us." The guard's voice was resonant with authority. She knew him as one who often avoided her company. Her warriors had also drawn their swords and were ready to do her bidding.

"I am your monarch and my father's command will not override my own wishes. You must return to my father and tell him I do my own will."

"My Lady—" the guard began but she cut him off.

"I am your queen, not your lady! Retreat to the castle by order of your queen," she commanded.

Though the evening was growing on them and her condition brought its weariness, Maab held herself straight and glared with fiery green eyes. The king's men hesitated till the lead warrior spoke again.

"Then we have been ordered to bring you back by force." He lifted his sword to signal their attack on the queen's protectors when she suddenly raised her face to the sky and released a long chilling howl that echoed into the forest behind them.

The Followers emerged from the dark trees with a ferocious snarling cacophony, causing all the horses to twist and stomp and throw some riders from their saddles. Though the beasts' bodies were the form of distorted wolves with hulking shoulders, their faces were grotesquely human baring canine teeth that protruded outside their lower black lips. Three of the beasts leapt onto the king's fallen guards until Maab called them off.

"Followers, stand by me!" she shouted once, then again till they obeyed. The fallen guards were helped back onto their horses. "Now you must retreat to my father and tell him to leave me to my business!"

The lead head guard gazed with astonishment at the attacking beasts who now stood encircling their mistress like guard dogs. But these were not dogs. Their long angular jaws pulled into a threatening grimace. Their wolfen shoulders twitched where they thrust upward from long sinewy necks. The guard waved his hand toward the castle indicating they were to withdraw. Maab watched them go and her child stirred inside her. She glanced around at her own warriors who were watching the Followers with caution.

"Fear them not. They follow my command."

"My Queen," Morleck began, "are these not the beasts...the very beasts that killed your mother and husband?"

She looked deep into his dark eyes and, for the first time, she knew the path she had chosen. Hers was a path of darkened terror and beastly mystery. She had not wanted her husband to die. Her only intention was to introduce him to the Followers, to reveal to him her power. But one of them took too much interest in his flesh, the same rogue beast that killed the queen in the previous year. She controlled the silver-maned rogue now, and she exploited his influence over the pack.

But there was a quiet voice insider her that still had doubts. It was the voice of the girl she had once been, Maab was sure, a child left behind long ago.

Now she knew why the necromancer had heeded her summons. He sensed her kindred soul, her obsession with death, but not the death that could release a soul to journey to its next sojourn, but the death that hovered in its lost and now forbidden world, held captive by the jealous memory of those the dead had left behind. Her body tingled at the thought of entering their ghostly realm where Armenthraal held them. It was there she would meet and speak with her husband.

"To the river," she ordered. "Armenthraal awaits."

She knew none of the men dared cross her and though the beasts held back from her as she rode to the river, she could see the fear that still lingered in her men's demeanor. She would assure them and gain full support from all the warriors in time, but for now she had a meeting to attend.

As they reached the long pier that thrust into the depths of the River Shryd, she saw the slow, enshrouded approach of Armenthraal's ghostly vessel. The red haze that surrounded its angular shape seemed to propel it along—a slow, menacing propulsion made from some unknown magic. The masts rose like dead, limbless trees. There were no sails.

"Wait for me on the shore. I do not know how long I will be, Morleck." She turned and began deliberately walking the length of the floating pier as the tall vessel touched the docking pilings. The fresh smells of the river's edge became engulfed with the scent of decay. The songs of the night birds fell silent and the song that replaced them was a repeating dirge rising from the ship. The baby stirred inside her again with a sudden insistence. She saw her husband's face in the swirling red haze.

Had the necromancer known her desires all along?

Her heart began racing. She had defied her father and set the ravaging beasts on his men—her men. What was she hoping to accomplish in this summoning? Would she really be able to speak with her dead husband? Would she meet her mother?

As though by cue, Armenthraal appeared. She did not see him disembark, but instead saw a thick cone of red haze that snaked from the ship's hull and onto the pier in front of her. He stood in its midst as straight and tall as an ancient conifer. He was draped in a deep purple cloak, so he appeared as a statue with his arms concealed and his head rising from the cloak as though carved in dark stone. His eyes glowed red, and he held her gaze until she spoke.

"Lord Armenthraal of Chalruck. I welcome you to my realm."

She felt the power of her words but could not hide the dread she began to feel. Her child kicked hard, and she flinched. The necromancer focused on her full stomach. His silence since his appearance made her skin chill as though winter stole into her veins.

"No matter where my ship docks, I am in my realm." He stepped toward her, but Maab could discern no foot movement. He seemed to float toward her and stopped at arm's length. "What do you ask of me? Why summon me?"

Maab saw again her husband's face in the red vapor and longed for him as never before.

"I wish to speak to my husband, who is among the dead these past two months."

Armenthraal's silence sent a vibration into the river and as Maab glanced down, its course seemed to reverse. "You are with his child?" His voice was like a slow creeping thunderstorm.

"I am. I wish my husband to know his son."

"You know it is a son?"

"It is a son. I know."

"You see as I see—into darkness."

His words shocked her, and she began feeling more pain than she wished to experience in this meeting. She held her middle in an attempt to quiet the child.

"There is a cost for such desires," he said, stepping closer to her.

She watched a red haze drift from his flared nostrils. The smell of death surrounded her, and she began to regret her chosen path and that she had not listened to her father. Would her husband want to speak with her now? Would he even recognize her? Maab gathered as much courage as she could muster. She glanced back to the riverbank where she had left her warriors but could not see through the dense red haze.

"I wish only to speak—" A sharp pain clutched her, and she gasped for air, nearly falling to her knees.

"Your time is near," Armenthraal droned as though he had ordered it to be so.

"No," Maab said. "No, it is not to be till the next early moon." Her pain subsided and she breathed deeply. "I only want to speak to my husband."

"There is a cost," Armenthraal repeated.

"Anything you ask. I am queen. I have riches, lands—"

"And I need nothing of this sort."

"Then what can I offer you? I need to speak to my husband. Name your price!"

But the pain returned and this time she fell to her knees and bent over, wrapping her arms around her abdomen. When she straightened again, an old woman stood beside the necromancer, her face hidden by a large cowl, her thin body shrouded in a grey tunic.

Terror sank into Maab's gut. She had never known terror. She commanded half-human beasts, more than a thousand broad-statured warriors, a kingdom with wealth and reputation. Yet now she felt powerless, alone and in terror. She waited, masking her fear with a determined face.

Armenthraal nodded to the old woman, who took one step toward Maab. Her voice was like an echo from some distant canyon.

"Your child comes soon, my Queen. He can be your offering, and I can help you birth him. I am death's midwife, though I have also served the living. The Lord Armenthraal transforms precious life into productive death." She reached her thin hand toward Maab's, but the queen stepped back, not fooled by the old woman's kind demeanor.

"No! That is not my offer! I have not come here to trade my child for your magic. Name another price! I have great wealth to offer you."

Maab's courage was restored as she sought to protect her child. The old woman stepped back to the necromancer's side like a chided dog.

Armenthraal opened his cloak where images swirled inside revealing jewels and vast lands filled with unimaginable wealth. "As I have said, I have no need of these things. They are all at my bidding." He turned like a retreating storm and moved toward his ship and stopped at the ladder. "And so it appears our meeting ends fruitless."

"Tell me, Lord of Chalruck," Maab cried out in desperation. "What can I give you in return for my husband's voice?"

"Only that which no one else possesses. Only that which stirs in your womb."

"I cannot give you my son."

"You can."

"I will not."

"That is different. You will not." He turned back to his ship and Maab noticed the old woman was gone. "If you have a will to resist my offer, then that will could be altered by stepping into my world. Follow after me to the place where I will lead. In the bowels of my ship there are many who await conversation with those left behind. There you will hear your husband's voice. You may listen at no cost. You may only listen. If you speak to him, your child is mine. You will have no choice inside my ship."

The necromancer floated upward onto his deck, and Maab quickly followed, climbing the short ladder behind him as though pulled by his energy. Her baby kicked hard again. And again. She placed her hand on her stomach when she reached the deck where Armenthraal stood beside the gaping entrance to the lower decks.

"Will I see others in this place?" she asked, fearing the answer.

"You will see into the eyes of only those who wish to speak to you. All the rest keep their eyes shut tight, fearing my gaze."

Maab thought of her mother. *Would she want to speak to me?* She wondered. *Could I hear both her and my husband? And how can I resist speaking when I see him?* She pushed against the strong urge to turn and run from this terror and Armenthraal's grisly influence over the dead. Yet as Armenthraal descended, her obsession took control, and she followed with no further hesitation.

The decks below were not in darkness, as she suspected. Rather, an ethereal light filled the cavernous room, and gradually she made out forms—people passing and talking, though she heard no voices—only their ashen lips moved. None of them looked at her, and what she found most surprising was their nakedness and their tightly closed eyes. Their skin was not that of a living man or woman, but the skin of one who lay dead on a bier. Their closed eyes were lifeless, and she avoided looking into them. She guessed there were hundreds trapped here on these ominous decks of death. She stayed close behind her guide till they reached what she believed would be the prow of the ship where a raised dais stood. Armenthraal stepped up onto the higher platform, turned, and addressed the ghostly crowd.

"My friends, my friends. We have a visitor who desires a word with one among you. Someone with whom she had a relationship...till he joined us here. This is Maab, Queen of the Shrydland, and she plays with death as I do."

The phantoms had stopped and stood as still as a breathless sea, their faces turned toward Maab. Her child kicked at her as though insisting she run from this death place before it was too late. But she had come this far. She breathed in determination and peered around the room, willing herself to focus on the faces of the dead. She did not see her husband. She was tempted to call his name, but she held her tongue and waited, gently rubbing her womb trying her best to sooth her child...and herself.

"My wife."

His voice was as she remembered, but it was only an echo, and it carried no emotion. She looked again into the crowd of blank, staring faces, the ethereal light making them appear like nightmarish demons.

"Why do you come here, my wife?"

She glanced at Armenthraal who nodded slowly, his red eyes glowing in anticipation. She could not answer.

"Our child that you carry does not belong here."

Then he appeared. Her forlorn, lost love. His face was clearer than any of the others, and his open eyes stared into hers as though to condemn her. His face was as it was when he lived, but the color had faded, and it was emotionless.

Tears welled up but she would not speak.

"My daughter." Her mother appeared next in a sudden flash of intense light. "Why do you come among the dead, with this beast who holds us captive here in his ship, feeding his voracious hunger for the wisdom of death while we wither under his watch? Do you not remember the story I told you as a child?"

Maab glanced at Armenthraal, who nodded again. Yes, she had forgotten the story till now. But in the presence of her dead mother and the death-slaver, the myth rang true. Yes, that's what he was. The captive dead served to sate Armenthraal's necromantic hunger. This was no haven for them. And there was no path for them to journey on from the life they knew. They were trapped. They had lost their way, and their will, and he was able to exploit their weakness. But she also remembered the part of the story where the death-slavers had once been cleansed from the Shrydland by her ancestors.

"Are you truly a man of your word, Lord of Chalruck?" she asked with a sudden awareness.

"My word is as true as death."

"Then I will do as you said and will not speak to my husband." She stepped through the throng and stood between her mother and her husband. They stood stationary, unable to touch her. "Mother, I come because I wanted to speak again to my husband and to hear his voice. Our child is nearly born, and I want to tell him that I will always keep his memory alive in our son's heart as he grows."

Maab surprised herself with her own sudden announcement. Until this moment she did not know what she wanted to say to her husband. Her mother's shrouded head raised slightly in acknowledgement.

"Your husband hears your words for him, spoken to me, my daughter."

"You speak to her, Queen of the Shrydland!" Armenthraal bellowed, causing the walls of the ship to shudder.

Maab turned back to him. "Yes, Armenthraal, to my mother but not to my husband as you had forbidden. I will keep our child. You cannot take him!"

"You play with my words. To speak to any who are dead is to trade your life or the life of your child with me!"

"Go, child! Go!" her mother said deep inside her mind. "Run from here, or my grandson will live in this hell for eternity."

"No one needs to live here, or die here, Mother. The Queen of the Shrydland does not run, not even from a death-slaver's threats." She turned and saw he was moving toward her, his arms outstretched.

"Run, my wife! Run from this place!"

Yet she did not relent. Instead, she raised her voice into the cavernous haze. "Open your eyes, dead ones! This is not your final home! This sorcerer-demon has entrapped you to serve his needs, but he does not possess you unless you allow it. And you have allowed it! He deceives you! Open your eyes, dead ones! Look on your captor!"

Suddenly the crowd began to do as she suggested, rubbing at their eyes as though waking from a long sleep. Opening their heavy lids so long closed, their eyes turned clear, and they looked toward Armenthraal. The necromancer stopped in his advance on Maab.

"My dead friends, pay no heed to this woman's lies. I give you safety in your death!" He brought his arm high to shield his face from the light that emanated from the dead ones' gaze.

"Cry out your names, Dead Ones!" Maab shouted. "Cry out the names of those you left behind. Bid them farewell and continue the journey where next you take form and live again. Fly to your heights, Dead Ones! Fly to your heights!"

As if they were an army responding to a command, the horde of dead transformed into various colored shades and then rose as one whirlwind of rainbow light into the night sky above them, a warm wind following as they ascended. A soft hush fell on the empty room where the throng once stood.

Maab was alone with Armenthraal in the dark lower deck. The ethereal hue was gone. Her mother and husband were gone. The necromancer slowly took his arm from his eyes and gazed into hers. His eyes no longer glowed red. He appeared as a defeated king.

"I will leave you to your ship, Lord Armenthraal. I would ask that you return to Chalruck tonight." As she ascended the ladder to the upper deck, she stopped and turned back to him. "I came here heavy in grief and obsessed with your world of dark magic. I was filled with a determination to speak with my husband and knew you had access to his existence beyond the grave— and my mother's. It is so. You have access, but you have taken far too much advantage of this access and have twisted it to serve you alone." She placed her hand on her stomach, and her child stirred calmly inside her. "Your threat to take my child was your mistake."

"I am not finished," Armenthraal growled menacingly.

"You are finished here, Dark Lord of Chalruck. Now you may go and allow the light to replace the shadow where your ship moors." She climbed onto the deck to the floating pier.

Maab was soon greeted by Morleck and her other warriors.

"My Queen! We saw the most astounding magic rising from this vessel, and the noise of the music was deafening. Did you hear it?" Morleck looked at her with a new respect. "My Queen? Forgive me, but your face…" She was mildly amused at his perplexed gaze. "It is changed."

"More than my face, dear Morleck. Yes, I heard the music, and saw it."

She allowed him to take her arm and lead her to her waiting horse. When she mounted, she paused and watched Armenthraal's eerie vessel pull away from the pier and disappear into the night. A soft golden haze remained where the ship had been moored. Maab hoped Armenthraal was only a lone remnant of his kind, but she knew in this instance, she had done her ancestors proud.

"Are the Followers still near?" she asked.

"They were here, my Queen, but when the magic appeared with its music, they disappeared quietly into the forest."

She nodded, knowing they would come at her command when needed. And she knew they would not attack another Shrydlander.

"Send word ahead to my father that I return with this new day. Tell him Queen Maab would have council with him, that she wishes to learn from him." She turned again to where the golden haze still hovered on the quiet current. "Tell him I found his daughter, and she returns to him."

THE END

Into the Forest

by Douglas W.T. Smith

A man doesn't run away into the forest. He stands by his family against all the odds that are thrown at them.

Jaeden crouched behind a fallen log and aimed at the boar, one eye staring down the arrow shaft, the other closed. His last meal was two days ago, and it had only been maple seeds and elderberries. He'd been stalking this particular boar since dawn, but now, as the sun hid behind rumbling storm clouds, he was running out of time.

His father's words still echoed in his thoughts.

Jaeden stared at the boar, which was absentmindedly digging its long nose and tusks into a tree burrow, wiggling its rear as it gouged out a hole. In the last week, Jaeden had learned to be quiet and listen to the woods' noises. At first, every move he'd made reverberated through the forest like an ogre's crashing foot stomps. Eventually, he learned to be one with his surroundings, and listening to the other wanderers of the forest, Jaeden became aware of his footprints, his steamy breath, and his human scent.

A soft winter breeze drifted between the trees, carrying the scent of damp moss and wet maple. Shivers ran down Jaeden's back, and the hairs on his arm rose to meet the cold. He had prepared for a possible turn in the weather, having donned his thick woolen cloak and leather boots before leaving home, but he hadn't prepared himself for such a long journey.

His father had always told him to stay in Ettenhun, but after the man's death, Jaeden spent more time in the forest. He didn't want to attend his father's burial service. He wanted to be away from his deranged mother and away from the chaotic outside world of kings and castles. But somehow, his father's words had a way of creeping up on him, like the crisp wind. They slithered deep under his skin and chilled his bones.

Jaeden took a deep breath and let his arrow soar. The shot hissed forward, blue tail feathers twisting through the air. He watched it arc down towards an unaware target, finally skimming off the boar's back into the closest tree, disappearing out of sight. The boar squealed and fled across a nearby shallow stream and into the trees.

Without pausing to reflect or search for his arrow, Jaeden chased after the animal. He knew he still had one left. His strides were larger than most men, allowing him to keep pace with the beast. The forest tried its best to slow him down, but Jaeden charged through. The cold, damp soil with fallen leaves slid under his quick footsteps as he sprinted after his prey, jumping over twisted twigs, rocks, leaping across the shallow stream. His determination propelled him onward, but he could not keep the pace up for long. Already, his arms and legs burned with exhaustion, his empty stomach groaned.

The boar pounded ahead, dodging grasping branches and leaping over moss-covered logs. Jaeden began to close the gap, lengthening his strides. The boar ducked under a hanging log. Jaeden jumped on top of trunk and halted, watching the animal flee for its life. Jaeden closed one eye, took a deep breath, grabbed an arrow from his quiver, and stretched the bowstring back. His chest expanded, still holding his breath, watching the boar fade into the shadows of the forest. Raindrops dripped down from the overhanging trees, landing on his hair, tickling and irritating him. Heavier drops tapped on his cloak and fell onto his hand as he aimed steadily at the boar.

He released his last arrow.

It glided through the air and struck true. The wild boar tumbled to the ground, disappearing into the underbrush.

Jaeden exhaled with relief and dropped from the log. He snuck up on the animal, knowing that with its last ounce of life it could strike at him. He noticed a streak of blood stretching out into the shrubs. He followed it further into the forest, eying the blood smeared on the ground, holding his bow with both hands, ready to strike.

As he followed the small stream of blood, thunderous clouds rumbled above him. Rain showered down. Blood ran across the rocks and leaf-covered ground. He followed the trace before it disappeared.

Ducking under a low hanging oak branch, he emerged to gaze at an enormous banyan tree. Its thick roots stretched out further into the forest, and between the limbs were dark crevices. Next to one of the roots was the boar. It was spread across the ground, staring at one of the openings, lungs rising and falling with deep but ragged breaths. Jaeden glanced at the arrow through its leg. The shot had ripped through the limb, and the boar's dash through the woods had only worsened the damage. A stream of blood merged with the rain and streamed down into a shallow puddle.

Jaeden carefully approached the boar with his hands out, showing the animal he didn't intend it any further harm. He crept up and crouched down, putting his bow over his shoulder. He wanted to pull the arrow out, wanted to put the beast out of its misery, but the boar stared at him, grunting with each painful breath. Raindrops thudded onto its body and ran down its cheek. It almost seemed as if it were crying.

A soft cry came from under the tree roots, and Jaeden lifted his gaze. A sounder of young boars crept out from the shadows, sniffing the air.

At that moment, Jaeden shuffled backward. The sight of the young boars watching what was clearly their mother stole his breath. The raindrops turned to tears, running down his face. He tried to control his wild emotions, taking short, ragged breaths, but he couldn't stop himself. The soft cries and snorting noises of the young pups clenched his heart. He watched as they all lay down beside the struggling sow—without their mother, nature would soon claim them, too.

He had thought he could do anything to survive. Almost anything. Not this. He could not be proud of this. What was he even doing out here?

Jaeden stepped back from the grim scene. Maybe it the sadness stirring in him came from memories of his father, or perhaps he genuinely cared about this animal and regretted taking the life of another parent, causing another to suffer as he did.

Jaeden took off his cloak and tossed it over the injured boar, leaning onto it. The infants dashed back into the cave as Jaeden wrestled the sow. It grunted and kicked its leg, thrashing about to throw him off but he pressed his chest down on its torso and held its neck down. The wild animal whined and thrashed, and Jaeden forced it to the ground, gripping the arrowhead. He snapped it off and pulled it through its leg. The boar squirmed and let out a piercing cry. The children returned their cries from the shadows. Jaeden pulled out the other end of the arrow and threw it to the ground. He leaped off the boar. It rolled out of the cloak, limping off to its children.

After some time, it appeared to Jaeden the boar would be fine. He picked up his cloak and left the family to rejoice in unity.

The sun appeared from the stormy clouds, shining in the forest, lighting up a brilliant spectrum of greens. Before the sun faded, consumed by another passing storm, Jaeden wiped the tear from his cheek and changed his path to follow the glistening sun ray.

He stands by his family, against all the odds that are thrown at them. Jaeden smiled, his father's words warming his soul, as he headed off in the direction of Ettenhun.

THE END

The Exile

by Nikola Chalakov

The ropes fixed Bea's tender arms tight to the upper end of the bed. Panic was slowly creeping in. She needed to double her efforts to escape. Bea knew she had to hurry, but spells never came naturally to her under pressure. She stared at the smoked stone ceiling while her mind drifted to thoughts of cedar and grapefruit, their soft scent floating around the narrow room. She found herself thinking of it instead of a spell she could use to free herself. The magical words would be of no use anyway—the silk cloth stuffed in her mouth prevented her from speaking.

She exerted all her strength, stirred her wrists, but she couldn't free herself. The spell was on the tip of her tongue, but everything was in vain.

"Time's up." She heard the familiar voice of her teacher, calm and exacting. "If this was for real, you'd be dead by now. Rozara, untie her. And make it quick. I have other things to do today."

Her friend with long black hair leaned over her, quickly removing the ropes and stepping back to let Bea sit on the bed. Bea finally took the cloth out of her mouth with relief and looked at her tutoress, who stood two steps away from her with folded arms.

The sorceress's slender figure was dressed in a long green dress, with a heart-shaped décolletage and elbow-length sleeves. There was no disappointment on her forever young face, but Bea knew what to expect.

"What went wrong?"

"Tutoress Melvida, I couldn't concentrate." Bea swallowed heavily. "I knew the spell, if only I could pronounce it..."

"There's no need to pronounce it. Didn't I show you? Your hands were tied, but your fingers were free. One precise movement would have summoned the right element."

"Just one more minute, and I would have done it!"

Instead of answering, Melvida looked at the big hourglass on the round table next to her. Then she gave a slight sigh, rubbing her square chin.

"One day, outside the castle, you might not have even a minute to spare."

Silence reigned, and none of the girls dared to break it. Bea and Rozara exchanged quick glances, waiting for the sorceress to say something.

"Well, that's enough for today. We'll try again tomorrow. With both of you." Melvida smoothed down the sleeves of her dress. "Rozara, get everything ready."

The black-haired girl took the hourglass, the ropes, and the silk cloth, seeing the tutoress out. She closed the door behind her back, and the two girls were left alone in the room. But just a moment later Melvida stood in the doorway again.

"You haven't forgotten that you must collect the fabric for my new dress, have you? Bea, you'll go alone. Rozara is still sick."

"I'm fine. I remembered the way carefully and—"

"I'm not blind, you're still faint. Stay here and gather your strength. You're going to need it." The sorceress's tone remained stern and uncompromising. "Explain to Bea how to get there. And you"—she pointed a finger at Bea—"I want you back in one hour. And don't talk to any bored guards along the way!"

"That's a pity," Bea said when their tutoress left. "It would have been fun to go for a stroll in the city together."

"There would be no time for that anyway. The shop isn't near."

"You're so gloomy!" Bea played with a tress of her blond hair. "Or you're just mad that you'll stay locked in here while I'm out!"

"A little bit. Do you know the way?"

"Refresh my memory. Wait! How do I look? Will you comb my hair?"

Bea quickly took the hairbrush hidden under her pillow and handed it to her friend. They both sat on the bed. There were no chairs in the room. Apart from the beds and the table there was only a modest wardrobe.

"Straight ahead along the main street after the square. A right turn at the two-story inn. And then?"

"You must reach several large flower shops," Rozara replied while diligently combing Bea's lustrous tresses.

"Ah yes, I remember! Isn't that close to the academy?"

"The academy?"

"The military academy, stupid!" Bea laughed. "The one with the guardsmen. I should go have a look. I want to watch them train."

"I don't think the shop is in the same direction."

"You're such a bore! All right, where to after the flower shops?"

"There's a small square," Rozara said, pausing a moment to remember the way. "We've been there several times."

"Always with Melvida however."

"This time you'll be on your own, I'm sure you'll savor the moment. Once you're there, go left, the shop is a thousand feet ahead. The sign is round. It says *Fabrics from Stegya* or something like that."

"My mother has a dress from Stegya. They really make fabulous fabrics there!" Bea felt the hairbrush stopping moving for a moment and turned around. Rozara had bowed her head. "I'm sorry, I shouldn't have said that." Bea bit her lip and gently lifted her friend's chin with a finger. "Forgive me."

"It's all right. You know that I don't even remember my mother. How could I?"

"I know," Bea said softly. "Come here."

Bea hugged her friend and in the silence of the room listened to her breathing. She wasn't well indeed. Or something was troubling her.

"You'd better go." Rozara drew back. "You don't need any more combing."

"Do you want me to get you something from the outside? Some flowers at least? I know you love them. Which one is your favorite?"

"Lavender. But we have no vase."

"Doesn't matter, I'll take several sprays to put under your pillow." Bea stood up and smoothed down the folds of her plain, grey dress. "It will do you good."

"Could you first drop by the kitchen for some food?"

"Of course," Bea replied. "What do you want?"

"Not for me. A little boy usually hangs around those flower shops."

"There are all sorts of beggars in the streets."

"His name is Gilles," Rozara said with a smile. "He's an orphan, not a beggar. I promised to bring him something."

"My father taught me to stay away from such tramps." Bea stamped her foot.

"Please, Bea." Rozara was puppy-eyed with pleading. "It's important to me."

Bea smirked. "You like this boy."

"Are you making fun of me now?" Rozara asked in mocked anger.

"Of course, not." Bea put a hand on her friend's shoulder. "For you, I'll make an exception. I'll deliver your message." She winked.

"Ah..." Rozara paused. "Yes, right. I trust you can do it. And I promise Baron Tirs will not find out!"

Bea faked a sulky grimace but couldn't repress her smile for long. She left Rozara seated on the bed and went out in the corridor. She quickly reached the steep stone staircase, then a wider corridor that took her to the spacious kitchen, where a small army of cooks and maids prepared the food for all novices and sorceresses living in the castle.

The place was busy and noisy, as it always was, stuffy despite the windows open wide. Above the tables hovered the smell of various spices which Bea couldn't recognize.

Nobody paid attention to her. It was time to cook dinner, and everyone was hard at work. Apparently, tonight's meal was venison. Bea thoroughly enjoyed the dish and reminded herself not to miss it as she looked around for something to bring to the boy. She chose the last piece of what had been a large wheel of cheese and stuffed it in a small bag together with a warm hunk of bread.

She escaped the kitchen before her dress totally absorbed the scents from the cauldrons, reaching the courtyard along another staircase. She strode across it, stopping only to greet two sorceresses with a slight bow. She recognized Ignis, with her red hair to the shoulders and her warrior-like northerner's face. The other one she hadn't met before. The woman wore a cloak with an embroidered silver moon, and it seemed that she had just arrived from a long journey.

They walked past her deep in conversation, and Bea continued on her way to the massive gate separating the castle's courtyard from the square. It was wide open. Beyond it stood Adarna, the capital of Tirilia. It was a place the novices of the Circle of Moonlight seldom got the chance to saunter without supervision or a task to carry out.

Today, Bea had two. First, she was going to do her friend's weird errand. Such whims occurred to Rozara from time to time. Bea just hoped the boy would really be there, as she had no desire whatsoever to look for him in the streets.

The castle and the oval square in front of it were now behind her back. A stream of people soon engulfed her as Bea began to walk among stuck-up tradesmen in austere clothes, hurrying servants in liveries in all kinds of colors, and swaggering officers in dark-green uniforms. Noblemen stared at the young ladies who were out on this fine day to show off their new glamorous dresses. A lonely rider carefully made his way through the throng. Bea also noticed in the distance a couple of novices she presumed to be from the Order of Ouroboros, but they disappeared in a side-street before she could have a better look at the crest on their cloaks.

Engrossed by the vibrant multitude, and by the various perfumes, trinkets and useless souvenirs from the capital shops, Bea almost missed the inn where she had to turn right. The military academy was in the opposite direction. Once again, she wouldn't be able to watch the boys whacking each other with wooden swords.

She heaved a sigh and moved her bag into her other hand. If only Rozara were here, she could have at least grumbled to her. Bea didn't walk for long before coming upon the flower shops. There was no way she could miss them—three wide, single-story buildings of blackened stone, covered with countless flowerpots and baskets holding all sorts of flowers. Roses, chrysanthemums, buttercups, and tulips—their colors flowed like a rainbow, while the soft summer breeze carried their fragrances down the street. Bea clearly distinguished the familiar sweet scent of gardenia, which sometimes floated along some of the castle corridors.

She picked up some lavender from a burnished cauldron then drew back to make room for two chatty ladies arguing how long different sorts of hortensia lasted. Passers-by often stopped at the front, some entered, others admired from the street. A boy in tidy, modest clothes hung around the ladies. He was thin and had tousled brown hair. Bea smiled. She was certain this was Rozara's homeless friend Gilles.

She was about to approach him right away, but the manner in which he was looking at the flowerpots in front of the nearest shop made her pause. She wasn't particularly good at spells yet, but she remembered one of Melvida's key lessons. *A good sorceress is an observant one.*

And now she could see that the boy was pretending. He wasn't interested in the flowers but in a distracted courtier in flamboyant tunic, who was just going out with a large basket of peonies in his hands. Gilles inconspicuously passed by him and snatched the purse from his belt with an adroit movement of his hand. He shoved it in his pocket and walked away with a relaxed gait.

Gilles was coming straight towards Bea. He smiled to her when their stares met and tried to continue down the street, but she stood in his way.

"I saw you, Gilles," she said quietly. "You're good but not perfect."

His eyes widened a bit, but the smile didn't leave his lips.

"You saw nothing. Did Boudock sent you? You're new, aren't you?"

"You're mistaking me for someone, it seems. Rozara sent me. I'm a friend of hers."

"Ah, say no more! Come with me."

She warily followed. Apparently, he wanted to put some more distance between himself and the previous owner of the purse. He led her in front of a small bakery, though he had no intention to buy anything.

It didn't take long for Bea to guess his plans. "Isn't one purse enough for you?"

"You don't understand a thing. What did you say your name was?"

"Bea Tirs. This is for you, from Rozara." She pushed the bag into his arms. "Even though you can buy some for yourself."

The boy opened it and immediately took a bite of the cheese. "You're doing fine there, at the circle," he said with his mouth full. "You just loll about, and they feed you well."

"I wish it was so." She laughed. "And you, when did you become a pickpocket?"

"I had to. And it's fun, too."

"Don't worry, I won't turn you in. Rozara would get angry with me."

"I know. Otherwise, you would already be screaming, *Guards, guards!*"

"They will catch you eventually," Bea warned, "and you'll be flogged. That's what my father does with thieves."

"I bet I can grab his purse, too, without him noticing! Do you want me to show you something?"

Bea was about to retort, but the young pickpocket tugged at her arm. Without resisting, she followed him to a narrow back alley. Gilles rushed with his short legs and confidently avoided the empty crates and barrels left in the road by the adjacent taverns. The fabric for Melvida's dress was getting further away with every step.

"Wait!" At last Bea made him stop for a moment. "There's something I must take care of."

"That can wait. Come on. You'll like it!"

"First, I have to collect something from a shop nearby."

"We'll go together. Do you promise to come with me afterwards?"

"I give you my sorceress's word." Bea was relieved when Gilles ceased bouncing and tugging at her arm.

They set out for Bea's objective and, after a short while wandering around the side-streets, found themselves on the main street underneath a heavy wooden sign that read *Fabrics from Stegya*. The shop was decorated by purple curtains with big tassels. The polished door was wide open.

"Wait here." Bea let go of the boy's hand. "I have to collect something. I won't be long."

"Leave it to me," Gilles said with a mischievous grin.

"Are you insane? They won't give it to you."

"Are you sure? Just tell me what it is and wait here."

The boy looked at her with his big brown eyes, and Bea could feel he was full of confidence. She decided to make him happy. At worst, he would get a slap in the face, and they would kick him outside.

"All right. Fabric for a dress. For Melvida of the Circle. Rozara ordered it. Got it?"

Without answering, Gilles bolted inside. Bea didn't mind being left alone for a short while, and she turned her attention to the lavender. It had a soothing scent, indeed. Tonight, she and Rozara would sleep tight and until late in the morning. That is, if their tutoress doesn't show up too early.

The calm didn't last long.

Gilles came back with a leap and a large package of silk taffeta, tied up with a twine of silver threads. "Got anything to say?" He handed it to her with a triumphant expression.

"You carry it for now. I still can't believe it! You don't look like a page of the Circle at all..."

"Now that that's done. Come on, this way!"

She had promised, so she now followed him. Neither the fabric nor the bag of food seemed to slow down his pace one bit. Fortunately, her stride was longer.

Soon they had left the streets Bea was familiar with, and she realized they were headed towards the western side of Adarna. The capital was large, even compared to many other cities, or so she had heard. Though, being constantly under the vigilant stare of their strict tutoress made it impossible for Bea and the other novices to verify. And she wanted to. The pulse of the city attracted her more and more with every passing day of seclusion at the castle.

However, she soon found this side of Adarna to not be the beautiful, clean, fragrant place of her dreams. The stone houses became wooden. Some were rather derelict. The ladies in ornate dresses and the bumptious noblemen disappeared, replaced by people in much more modest, even shabby clothes. But this did not prevent some of them from laughing. Others had loud conversations, while a few walked silently, gazing at this new girl with long blond hair.

Bea regretted not having Rozara with her. Her friend could manage easier in a quarter such as this. Instead, Bea's only guide was little Gilles. Fortunately, the boy seemed to know exactly where he was going and many of the passers-by greeted him.

"When are we going to play cards again?" a stumpy, short-bearded roughneck came forward to say.

"Save some gold griffins first," Gilles replied.

"Who's your new friend?" asked a woman dragging along a heavy head of cabbage.

"She's from the royal court!"

"Hey, that's a lie!" Bea turned her head to him in dismay.

"Don't spoil it then. Just smile and keep walking!"

Bea hastened forward, pursued by the whistles of a group of deadbeats sitting in circle around a big jug.

"I hope you're having fun," she whispered to the boy through her teeth, "because I'm not. How long are we going to walk?"

"We're close now. First, we'll drop by over there."

He pointed at a tumbledown, one-story house some ways down yet another back alley. Gilles paused to give her the fabric. Then, instead for the door, he headed for a pile of planks in the corner. They were covered in dirt and rags. After making sure no one was watching, he pulled something out of the mess and stuffed it under his shirt, too fast for Bea to identify the object.

He didn't say a word to her. She didn't ask either and followed him silently, turning her head to the sky. The sun was close to the horizon. She hoped Rozara could somehow draw Melvida's attention away from her lateness. Still, she had to come back in time for dinner. If she wasn't there for it, her absence would not be unnoticed.

Bea was happy when then finally stopped in front of a large dark house and Gilles explained with a sign that they have reached their destination. She was beginning to get used to the cautiousness of the young thief and wasn't surprised when they went round and entered through a tiny door at the back of the building. It seemed that its proper function was to be used for bringing inside firewood, because it took them straight into a vast basement.

Gilles lit a rusty lantern, which hung on a chain from a beam in the middle of the room. In the light, Bea saw there was indeed some firewood inside, piled up in a corner. Everywhere else was a disarray of heaped up dressers, chests, and chairs. On them stood, gathering dust, an assortment of massive candlesticks, delicate statuettes, and small boxes, just like the ones in which Bea's mother, the baroness, kept the most precious jewelry of the house of Tirs.

"You've amassed quite a number of things." Bea put the fabric and the lavender on a chair that had ornate fretwork on the backrest. "How long did it take you?"

"I've been in Adarna for a year. Everything here belongs to Boudock. We're collecting it for him."

"What's your relation with this Boudock?"

"He sheltered me. I used to sleep in the streets."

Bea opened a box and gasped in surprise. "It's beautiful!"

Inside lay a silver bracelet, an emerald glimmered in its center. Gilles got on his toes and closed the box under her nose.

"Don't touch!" he hissed. "It's Boudock's. I told you."

"I don't know how much it is worth, but it's a lot!"

"A hundred griffins, probably."

"Apparently you know more about it than I do." Bea rubbed the beauty spot on her right cheek. "Why did you bring me here?"

From under his shirt the boy produced the thing he had picked up earlier. Removing a piece of cloth from around it, he showed it to her–a square box, about one hand wide. A necklace covered in diamonds gleamed in the light of the lantern. Bea had never seen one like it. It looked worthy of a countess at the royal court.

"Do you like it? Do something for me, and it will be yours. Boudock doesn't know about it."

"You want me to steal, don't you? It's a wonderful piece of jewelry, but I'm no thief."

"You won't have to steal anything. Just help me get into a certain house."

"Why?" Bea measured him with her eyes.

"Take a guess! Boudock is keen on getting some stuff from there. I have to bring it to him."

"What do you need me for? You're dexterous enough."

"That house..." Gilles bit his lip. "It's protected by magic. If you don't lead me through it, I'll get fried."

"So, that's it." Bea slapped her forehead. "You want to rob someone of the Order. Or the Circle, same thing. If they catch us, you'll rot in prison for life. And they could even behead me. It won't matter than my father is a baron."

"You're chicken!"

"I've got another idea." Bea kept her tone calm but assertive, not unlike that of her own tutoress. "You need better friends. You and I are going to the royal guard. They will take care of Boudock."

"No!" Gilles stamped his foot and hid the necklace underneath his shirt. "He's the only one who's going to help me."

Bea was beginning to lose patience, and her time was running out. The scent of the lavender reminded her that she needed to get back to the castle, soon. She couldn't stay with the young thief any longer. In the end, if it hadn't been for Rozara, she wouldn't have spoken to him at all. He wasn't her problem.

"What is he doing for you anyway?" She tried one last time to convince the boy. "He's using you! I'm leaving, and you'd better come with me."

She turned her back on Gilles to gather her things. As she considered whether she could find the way back without him, there came a loud creak above their heads, then a bang from a door slamming shut and heavy footsteps.

"It's him," the pickpocket whispered. "Hide, quickly!"

Bea would rather run out to the street, but she was far from the exit, and another door was already opening at the other end of the basement. She only had time to squat behind a big dresser covered in cobwebs. Gilles pushed a chair to conceal the path to her hiding place and turned to face the newcomers.

The first to step into the light of the lantern was a square-built man of average height with a rough face. He wore a cloak and a green bandana on his head. Bea assumed the man was in his forties, with a wrinkled high forehead and a menacing stare. His thuggish smile foreshadowed the worst.

Behind him stood two men Bea immediately identified as cut-throats, even though she had never met any bandits before. Their clothes were unkempt and worn out, yet the knives at their belts seemed perfectly sharp.

"You've returned early." The voice of the man with the cloak was hoarse and commanding. "Today's catch was a good one, I hope?"

Gilles quickly handed him the purse from the flower shop. The man tossed it up into the air and caught it again. The coins inside clinked.

"Is this all? Why aren't you on the streets to get some more?"

"I'll make up for it tomorrow, Boudock. I promise!"

"Listen, shorty, this simply won't do." The man gave the purse to one of his thugs and threw out his arms. "Do you realize how much money we are going to need to get you back home?"

"I'm doing my best—"

"A fortune! We'll need a nice ship. And some mercenaries. And money to bribe your brother's servants. Because what is he going to do if he catches you, remind me?"

"He'll kill me." Gilles bowed down his head.

"Exactly! So, if you really want to take his place someday, you should put more effort into it! Otherwise, you might end up the one wearing the iron mask."

The boy raised his chin, and Bea noticed a flash in his eyes. A chill went down her spine as she sensed the hatred burning in them.

"That's why you'll do as I say," Boudock went on. "Without me, you'll be in exile all your life."

Boudock crossed his muscular arms over his chest and began examining the haughty collection amassed in the hideout. His eyes glimmered with joy, like that of a dragon lolling atop a mound of treasure. Just like the dressers, the floor was covered in a thin layer of dust. Boudock's studied something on the floor then turned towards the small door to the street. The rough man rubbed his pointy chin.

"What's that smell? Gilles, you know you're not supposed to bring anyone here. Whose footprints are these?"

"Why, whose can they be? They're mine."

"Don't play me for a fool. Come over here, boy. Those are from shoes pointed at the front. These others are from yours. Lads, search for uninvited guests. Now!"

The two cut-throats started to push chairs aside and look behind the dressers. Bea bit her lip, choosing to reveal herself. She had to push aside the fear gripping her. Fear always takes your strength away, giving it to others.

"Who are you then?" Boudock examined her from head to toe with a crooked smile. "A friend of my little fellow?"

"Look, I don't know who you are, and I don't want to know." Bea's voice sounded far from the confidence she wanted to demonstrate.

"Don't be mad. We were just going for a walk." The boy shuffled his feet. "Besides, she could take part in—"

"I decide who takes part! She looks like a rich man's girl. What have you got there?"

Boudock stretched out his dirty hand, but Bea drew back. She stumbled on a chest, nearly tripping on the ground. The men laughed.

"Nothing of value to you." Bea collected the last threads of her self-control. "I'm leaving, because they'll be looking for me if I'm late."

"Is that so?" Boudock blocked her way. "Not so fast. Since you're here, you have to participate in our little undertaking. You need to pay for not keeping your nose out of other people's affairs."

"I can't... and I don't want to. I'm not interested in what you're doing. I'm with the Circle."

"You don't say? Usually, sorceresses find coming in our part of town to be beneath their dignity."

"I won't be back, and I won't tell the Guard about you."

"Don't you threaten me with the Guard, lass! We'll be out of here before they have even left their barracks!"

This time the laughter was quieter, more evil. Bea's time was running out and she couldn't think of a way to get past the three strong men.

"Look, if you do something for us, we'll forget about this incident." Boudock peered at her with judging eyes. "With some of your spells, we could get inside places once beyond our means."

"No, I can't..." Bea searched desperately for a path to the exit.

"If you're of no use to us, then, well...."

"Don't hurt her." Gilles grabbed the bigger man by the sleeve. "Her father is a baron!"

"Now we're talking!" A wicked smile once again crossed Boudock's face. "This means she's rich. She can buy herself out."

"Thanks, you little traitor," Bea hissed.

"Calm down, your ladyship." Boudock raised his hand with a wide smile. "Since you're here anyway, you'll be our guest until your father pays a ransom. How much would he give?"

Bea fell silent. Sweat dripped down her face as she frantically sought a way out. She could attack them with a spell, but if she failed, there would be no escaping their sharp knives.

"What is your father's name?" Boudock asked. "I'm certain he would gladly part with some modest amount of money to get his daughter back safe and sound. Let's say five hundred griffins?"

"The piece of jewelry Gilles is hiding from you under his shirt is worth more than that."

"How could you!" the boy shouted, his face pale in the lantern light. "Damn you!"

"You started it, fool!" she shouted back.

"I just want to get back home."

"Shut up, the both of you!" Boudock hit Gilles in the stomach. "Get her!"

His men pushed Bea back towards a dresser, while their leader searched the boy. He quickly found the necklace, then he slapped Gilles hard in the face, turning his attention to the glittering diamonds.

In the meantime, the thugs knocked Bea to her knees and snatched the roll of fabric from her hands. When they realized what it was, they threw it on the floor among the scattered lavender sprigs.

Bea saw that Boudock still had the necklace in one hand, a knife in the other. She had to overcome her uncertainty and act. She couldn't afford to wait for him to decide whose throat to slit first.

She summoned in her mind a destructive spell and raised her hand without rising from the dirty floor. The first word ringed out from her lips and echoed through the basement. She directed the magical blast at a rotten beam she noticed above their heads. A crash thundered. The beam broke and fell on one of the thugs. The entire house shook above their heads. At first, Boudock and his other henchman tried to come closer to her, but then decided it was safer to grab as much loot as possible and run away before the building would collapse.

Bea and Gilles were about to follow them through the door when a part of the upper floor fell down and blocked the exit, filling the air with thick dust. Bea was devastated. Her triumph was to be their doom, as her powerful spell got out of control.

As she stood petrified, Gilles grabbed her hand and lead her towards a dark corner of the basement. They frantically cleared a pile of rubble and revealed a secret way out. They left the hideout right as another wall was beginning to break into pieces.

Outside, the thugs were nowhere to be seen. Perhaps this close encounter with magic had made them flee without looking back. Cradled in Gilles's hands, Bea was surprised to see fabric she had to bring to her tutoress. Given the chance to grab anything in that room, the boy had chosen this. She seized it from him and held it tight to her chest. Then she gave him a fierce hug.

Bea wanted to get away from this place as quickly as possible. She headed in the direction of the main road, assuming that was the safest place to be at the moment.

She turned back to Gilles "Are you coming?"

The boy quickly followed her, and they got out in the street. A small group of curious onlookers had gathered to gawk at the crumbling building and now nimbly dispersed. It was growing dark, the last sunrays caressed the roofs and towers of Adarna.

"I've never seen anything like that," the boy looked her in the eyes. "You destroyed an entire building! You are a great sorceress."

"I'm not, but I have my moments. Now, can we agree that Boudock is an evil man?"

"Yes."

"And you don't want to cross his path ever again?"

Gilles nodded in agreement.

"Then come with me. A mutual friend of ours will be delighted to see you."

The way back took them longer as Bea felt exhausted from the spells. When they finally reached the castle and the heavy gate closed behind their backs, she used her last strength to bring the boy and the dirty fabric to the room she shared with Rozara.

The black-haired girl was still awake, waiting for them. Rozara greeted them with a wide smile and gave Gilles a hug.

"You two look like you've been in a mine," she said looking at the dirt on their clothes and faces.

"Pretty close," Bea mopped her brow. "It's a bad neighborhood."

"I know," Rozara said plainly. "I was hoping you would find Gilles and bring him here."

"You knew?" Bea scowled. "About Boudock?"

"I knew you could take care of it." Rozara smiled. "I have faith in you, even if you don't yet have faith in yourself."

"She was alone against three men and still made them run away like cowards." Gilles was brimming with excitement.

Rozara smiled at the boy, then turning to her friend, she put a hand on Bea's shoulder.

"See, when the time comes, magic flows through you naturally. I was certain you could do it."

THE END

The Bonds of Madness

by JM Williams

W AKE UP!...Wake up, Chari!"

Chari struggled to open his eyes. He felt the rough touch of stone on his skin, cold and wet. Seya was staring down at him, her thick pigtails bobbing along with frantic sobs. Around him, the chamber—an unfamiliar and unnerving place—was dark except for a few dim torches burning some distance away, the flames giving the weeping girl an ethereal presence.

"Chari, get up!" Seya cried, shaking him roughly.

As his eyes adjusted to the darkness, Chari saw several figures surrounding them, tense, swaying with anxiety, standing on hoofed feet. *Satyrs!* Red-furred goatmen with horns on their heads, and crooked legs that were stepping steadily forward. Vermin who had become increasingly violent towards the local villages. These held hooked blades in their hands, and they were closing in.

Chari braced himself on his large arms and rolled onto his knees. His leather armor creaked with the motion, as stone dust fell from his short black hair like dandruff. He found a sword lying close by and picked it up, readying himself for a fight. He felt the familiar grooves of the tree-shaped handle. It was his sword.

"You'll have no chance against them in your current state," a voice said to him.

Chari glanced around but saw no one hiding in the shadows. There was only himself and Seya, and the advancing satyrs.

"Give me control and I can save you," the voice said, this time more insistent.

"What?" Chari shouted.

The voice sounded close, but there was no one to speak it in the small, closed off chamber. A single exit lay in the distance, revealed by distant torchlight. It was blocked by the satyrs.

"Who are you?" Chari asked. "Where are you?"

"I'm in your head, fool," the voice said. *"Don't you remember our bargain?"*

"Bargain?" Chari struggled to make sense of the word. "What bargain?"

"Chari, who are you talking to?" Seya asked, her voice trembling. "The monsters are coming, Chari. Do something!"

"Now is not the time for talk," the voice echoed in Chari's head. *"I promised to lead you safely out of this cave. You promised me a place in your head for the journey. Now surrender your body, or we will all soon cease to be."*

Chari could not make sense of what he was hearing. But the idea of a promise felt vaguely familiar. The satyrs were almost on them now, cautious but advancing with deadly intent. One drew back its sword for an attack.

"Give me control!"

Chari hesitated. He felt a pressure in his mind, like something was trying to bore into his thoughts. His body jerked. His limbs started to move without his urging them to. It was a strange, unnerving sensation. Chari resisted. He saw the satyr's blade cutting through the air towards his face. Chari wanted to defend himself, but he could not move. He could only watch his impending doom in frozen horror.

Then his sword-bearing arm reached out, faster than Chari could have managed on his own. His sword collided with the satyr's, but instead of a mere parry, a wave of force shattered the enemy blade and sent the goatman tumbling backwards. Chari struggled to regain control of his body, but he could not affect a single movement.

Seya screamed and collapsed into a ball, hands over her ears.

In one movement, Chari's body jumped to its feet and charged the remaining satyrs. Chari could do nothing but watch. It was terrifying to be so out of control. He wanted to scream, but he could not pass a breath, could not make a sound. He was unable to move a single one of his own muscles, yet he still felt every repercussion of their actions. He felt the impact of every blow in his arms and wrists, felt the dizziness of the spins. The fighter controlling his body was better than he could ever hope to be, its every move flawless.

His sword arm spun and slashed and thrusted. His legs dipped and danced. His body spun around the enemy. A slash across the gut dropped one satyr to the ground. A twist on his heel and a thrust in the back ended another. A third approached from the left, and Chari's empty hand reached out, fingers pointed forward. Arcs of purple lightning shot from his fingertips into the satyr's face, causing its skin to sizzle and smoke, the creature's body convulsing on the ground. With a cavalier toss of his sword, a final beast fell to the stony floor, the blade embedded in its chest up to the hilt.

"It is done," the voice said weakly.

This time when Chari attempted to scream, the sound came out full, reverberating around the room. He shook his body, trying to free himself from the invisible puppet strings that controlled him. Then, hit by a surge of exhaustion, he fell to his knees. Surveying the carnage around him, he noticed there were five dead satyrs on the ground. Blood covered his hands and arms and clothes. Seya was on her knees in a corner, rocking back and forth.

"The monolith with hands of black!" she screamed.

"Seya!" Chari crawled to her side.

"Hands of red welcome him," Seya babbled. "Hands of blood!"

Chari took her by the shoulders and shook her. "Seya! Snap out of it!"

"Is this girl mad?" the voice asked.

"Yes!" Chari replied bluntly. "Sort of...Seya, look at me."

The girl's dark eyes opened. Her breathing slowed, and she stopped fidgeting.

"Brother!" she cried and wrapped her arms around him.

He returned the embrace, running his hand through her hair, now sticky with sweat. He sat there for a long while, holding her. Only half his size, the girl disappeared into his thick arms, her blond pigtails the only evidence of her presence. They twitched with sobbing.

"What have you done to us now, girl?" Chari said softly.

"I'm sorry," she said.

"It's okay. I'll get you out of here."

"Take me home, Chari."

The young man rose to his feet. He wandered around the dimly lit chamber until he found his sword, pulling it from a satyr corpse, looking the bloody metal over, checking for breaks or cracks. Satisfied the blade had survived the previous battle, he returned to Seya and offered the girl his hand.

"We had a deal, swordsman," the strange voice said. *"I just saved your life. Now you must take me out of this cave."*

"Who in the five hells are you?" Chari said, his anger filling the dark room.

"Chari, who are you talking to?" Seya asked again.

"Why do you insist on using your feeble voice? I am in your head. I can hear your every thought."

"Who are you?" Chari asked with his mind's voice.

"That's better...We have already been introduced. Do you not remember?"

"Obviously I don't."

"Maybe the possession has strained your mind more than expected. You were unconscious for some time. It seems I must jolt your memory."

"Possession?"

"My name is Zajur. I am a...spirit. I have been trapped in this cave for centuries."

"And I promised to take you out?"

"Yes. In exchange for my protection. That was our bargain."

Chari hated the idea of being bound to a promise he could not remember making. But it seemed like he had little choice at the moment. He had no idea how to purge a wandering spirit from his mind. And the most important thing to do was to get out of the cave before more satyrs found them.

The most important thing was to protect Seya. That was the only thing that truly mattered.

With a wave, he ushered her forward. She took his hand firmly, ignoring the blood, burying her own tiny fingers into it. He noticed the blood stains on her sand-colored dress. It was a familiar sight. The implications of it hung in his head longer than he liked.

Refocusing his thoughts on the current danger, he led the girl through the far passage, out of the chamber. They passed by several more satyr bodies, and he assumed he must have been the one responsible for their current state. He had come looking for Seya; that much he remembered.

He was always finding himself in uncomfortable situations, always chasing after a girl who was apt to wander into dangerous places without a thought. The girl's disconnect from reality was a symptom of her sickness. It was the burden Chari had to bear. She was family. Though, he had never woken up in a cave with a fog over his memory—this was a frightening first. Seya must have run off into this cave during one of her fits, and he had come running after, dressed for a fight. The satyr's cave. So, this was where the cretins had been hiding these past months. But why?

The cavern was lit by small torches all the way through. The way they burned seemed somehow unnatural, with a blue tint to their light. When he passed one, the breeze given off by his movement did not seem to affect it. He reached out to touch it.

"Do not touch that flame," Zajur warned. *"It is not part of this world."*

"What does that mean?" Chari continued walking, testing the weight of the sword in his hand.

"This cavern is a gateway, a transition. We stand halfway between the land of the living and the nether realm."

"Is that why the satyrs are drawn here?"

"Perhaps. It is hard to say."

"And that's how you came here? From the nether realm?"

"Yes."

"And you want to pass into the land of the living?"

"Yes."

"Why?"

"That is none of your concern."

Chari stopped, anger rising up inside him again. Seya yanked on his hand, and he looked down at her.

"Are you okay, brother?" she asked. "You seem bothered by something. And you still didn't tell me who you were talking to."

"What is wrong with this girl?"

"Ever since she could talk, Seya has been prone to babbling and getting lost. It's why no one would take her in. A mad girl was too much of a burden."

"But you did."

Chari did not know how much he should tell the spirit, how much he could trust it. But it was inside his head, after all, and could probably dig out any answer it wished. And it might not be a good idea to anger a spirit with the power to control his body. Chari decided to be amicable.

"I understand her situation. I was orphaned, too, at a young age, when my own mother went mad. She killed herself. But it was a slow, painful death of years. She had

never recovered from my father's death. I never met the man, but the way my mother talked about him...She said he died at war, before I was born. I know what madness can do to a person. And I know about being alone. I never knew the beautiful, sane woman my father once loved. I never knew my father. I met Seya and saw how she was treated, remembered how my mother had been treated. This girl deserves better than that. Her sickness isn't her fault."

"She calls you brother."

"I'm not really her brother, no. She was too young to remember when I started caring for her. The easiest way to explain things was just to say we are siblings. In a way we are. I couldn't tell her that nobody in our village, any village, wanted her, wanted anything to do with her. She's too young to understand that sort of prejudice."

"Perhaps I could find the root of her madness."
"How?"

"Just put your hand on her head. It's...a spirit thing."

Chari was still unsure if he could trust Zajur, but he was also desperate for answers.

"Seya, my friend wants to examine you. He thinks he might be able to understand your sickness."

"Your friend? The one you've been talking to? You have a voice in your head, too, right?" She smiled at him.

Chari tried to smile back, but was disturbed by her comment. She looked him in the eyes and nodded. She trusted him. He hoped he would not betray that trust. Reluctantly, he placed his hand on the side of her face.

Seya's eyes went wide, and her mouth opened to scream. "The monolith with hands of black!" Her body began to shake. "Twist the blade and turn the key!"

Chari's hand grew hot, and he drew it back. The moment he did, Seya relaxed and her breathing slowed. Tears ran down the side of her face where his hand had left a glowing print. The amber light quickly faded.

"*She's been cursed,*" Zajur said. "*By the Mad God himself.*"

"*The Mad God? Why would the Nameless One care about Seya?*"

"*I cannot be sure. But the madness feeds her mind with visions, with compulsions.*"

"We need to get out of here," Chari said aloud.

He grabbed Seya by the hand and took off faster than before. He moved so quickly that he felt himself dragging her along. But the girl did not complain. By now, she was used to having her brother drag her away from all sorts of dark places. It had become routine.

Ahead, the cavern split into two paths.

"*Do you know the way?*" he asked the spirit.

"*I don't exactly have eyes of my own, do I? In the nether realm, I have true form. Here I am little more than a wisp of wind.*"

Not wanting to waste time, Chari took the right branch. Rounding a sharp corner, he almost crashed into an oblivious satyr. He stabbed it without a second thought. The sound of the creature's pike hitting the ground alerted its three comrades, which Chari had failed to notice. They spun around and charged. Chari pushed Seya behind him and gripped his sword in both hands, stepping forward.

The first satyr attacked with a downward sword-slash. Chari held his own sword up and parried the blow, shoving the goatman away with the momentum. Then he spun and buried his blade into the gut of a second slashing enemy. He pulled it out and shifted to the creature's side. He used the friction of the blade's release to drag the beast into the third attacker. It held its arms out in a feeble attempt to support its comrade, which gave Chari enough time to thrust his sword around the wounded satyr into the healthy one. The two fell to the ground together. The last one was soon on top of the pile.

"The monolith with hands of black!" Seya screamed as she ran back the way they came.

"Damn," Chari muttered, sprinting after her.

He came to the split in the path and stopped, straining to hear. The sound of running feet echoed from the second path, the one they had skipped by earlier. He dashed off after her, driving his legs as fast as he could manage.

Up ahead, he saw a small, shadowy figure disappear into a circle of light. The end of the tunnel was brightly lit, a mix of gold and white-blue lights flickering in a wide space. Chari continued forward, blinded by the glare.

As his eyes adjusted to the light, Chari could see he was in a large chamber, lit by blue torch fires and golden flames in ornate braziers. Three separate tunnels converged on this point and the chamber moved deep into the stone, away from the paths. At the far end, he saw an onyx-black statue. Tall and slender, with a pointed top, the monolith had an obscure figure carved into its front side. An old face and two bent arms protruded from the column. An altar was set before the statue, with a single offering plate. Seya was kneeling before it.

Chari moved forward, glancing cautiously down the other two paths and keeping his distance from the blue torches. As he approached Seya, a wild wind kicked up and stopped his advance. A bitter cold scratched at his skin, as a bluish shadow formed in the dust storm. The shadow grew in size, solidifying into a male figure that resembled the statue, the monolith still visible behind and through the figure's transparent image. The ghostly man's fingers and limbs were crooked, his hair unkempt and wild. He looked like a crazed hermit.

"Ahh, my vessel has finally arrived," the ghostly figure said, his deep voice real and physical, but distant. The sound filled the damp chamber, seeming to originate from everywhere, and from nowhere. "It sure took you long enough, girl. Last time I trust a child with complex navigation." The ghost chuckled loudly.

Chari raised his sword.

"And who might you be, big man?" The ghost said. "That's some nice meat on your bones, but is there anything inside that ridiculously big head of yours?"

The shadow reached out a hand in Chari's direction. Thunderous pain erupted in Chari's head, forcing him to his knees. His vision pulsed between shadow and spark.

"Zajur, the coward!" The shadow man shouted. "You little wretch, I was wondering where you'd gotten off to. What are you doing hiding in here? Well, I guess you *have* always preferred dark and empty spaces!"

Chari cried out in pain. "What is he talking about?" he said through gritted teeth.

"Oh? Little Zajur didn't tell you?" the ghost said mockingly. "My, my, what a shady, disloyal little servant he is."

"Servant?" Chari asked. "Your servant?"

"Of course!"

"And who are you?"

"Who am I?" the ghost said, putting a finger to his spectral head as if pondering the question. "Well, my name is...You know, I don't remember! I must be mad!" The ghost laughed again.

"The Mad God..." Chari said under his breath.

"Displeased to make your acquaintance, I'm sure," the Mad God said with a dramatic bow.

"If Zajur is your servant then—"

"He is a demon, of course. Isn't that just quaint?"

"Zajur, why didn't you tell me?" Chari said with his mind's voice.

"Would you have bargained with a demon? I only wish to be free of these bonds. Free from this madness."

"You know, it's not fair to speak behind someone's back. Zajur, you're such a gossip!" The Mad God's voice laughed in Chari's mind. Each devilish chuckle came with a ripple of pain.

"Get out of my head!" Chari shouted, shaking his head.

"Get out of my ritual chamber, boy," the Mad God said aloud, suddenly serious. "There is work to be done, and I will not have you getting in the way."

"Give me the girl," Chari said, pointing to Seya, "and we will leave you in peace. You can take your servant back."

"But you see," the Mad God began, "she is mine, and he is yours. You did make a bargain with the little miscreant. You can't just toss a demon aside when you see fit, my boy. And this little one"—he pointed to Seya—"has been mine, long before you ever started chasing her. What's mine is mine and what's yours is yours. No switch backs!" The ghost opened his arms in a welcoming gesture.

"Oh, look, the priest has arrived. Time for the little snip-snip!"

Chari spun around to see satyrs converging from each of the three tunnels. Dozens of them. The one leading the group was dressed in a sky-blue robe, quite unusual for a goatman. It held a curved knife in his hand.

"That's a ritual knife," Zajur said. *"I think they intend to offer Seya as a sacrifice to the Mad God, as a body for him to use to enter the land of the living. Her curse was meant to bring her here. One cut, that's all it will take."*

"Help me, Zajur!" Chari pleaded.

"I...cannot..."

"That little whelp has always been such a whiner," the Mad God's voice said in Chari's mind.

"I will not let you have her!" Chari screamed aloud.

"Hands of red welcome him. Hands of blood." Seya chanted, her body swaying.

Chari gripped his sword in both hands. Two lines of satyrs spilled around their priest protectively. One lunged at Chari with a pike. He batted it aside with a bracer-clad arm and stabbed it in the neck. A half-dozen more were on him in a moment. Chari focused all his attention on parrying their blows, on staying one step ahead of their attacks. There were too many.

As Chari clashed with an increasing number of the beasts, the priest stepped around the melee towards Seya. Chari would not let it touch her. Using the flat side of his blade, he knocked a nearby satyr on the side of the head, forcing it to bend forward. Chari climbed atop it and leapt off, landing in a roll and spinning up in front of the priest. He gutted the vile creature.

The ritual knife hit the ground with a clang and disappeared behind a stampede of hoofed feet. Chari once again found himself fighting more enemies than he could handle, the exhaustion seeping into his muscles like a poison.

"You know, the robes are just for show," the Mad God said. He put a hand to his mouth as if telling a secret. "If you ask me, these guys are all a bit dim. Get it? Were in a cave. Dim?" The ghost waited for a response that never came. "Fine, be that way. Good humor is an acquired taste. Just so you know, it doesn't matter who draws the girl's blood, just as long as it stains the blade. You can't kill all of these pitiful little creatures. Strength in numbers, as they say."

"Zajur, help me!"

One satyr leaned forward, slashing downwards at Chari with a curved sword, while another thrust with a pike. Chari stepped to the side, diverting the pike into the swordfighter, and dragging its blade arm down across the pikeman. Something sharp stung his side, and he rolled away, shoving two goatmen aside as he moved. Putting a hand to his back, he discovered a deep, gushing pike wound. In the crowd of satyrs, he saw a red hand grasp the ritual blade.

There were too many for Chari to fight. His strength was spent, and he was losing blood from several wounds. He fell to his knees.

"Zajur, help me."

"I cannot defy my master."

"I always knew you were a coward, little Zajur," the Mad God said. *"Always the weakest of your brothers."*

"We had a bargain!" Chari bellowed.

The chamber filled with the dull clomps of hoofed feet. Satyrs drew in on Chari from all sides, and a smaller group marched towards the collapsed girl at the altar. Chari could do nothing. His body was crippled by fatigue. The last bits of his strength drained away with each drop of blood from the pike wound. Part of him had known Seya might lead him to a place he could not escape, but that had never stopped him from following. Even now, he worried for her more than himself, for the oblivious girl now kneeling before a demonic altar.

Suddenly, energy and tension rippled across his body. Chari's hand opened without his bidding, dropping the sword. Once again, he was losing control of his body. This time he surrendered to it completely.

He let the demon take over.

"Let me show you how weak I am!" Zajur shouted through Chari's voice.

Chari felt his hands move outward, as swords swung down on him from several directions. A pulse of light and force surged out, sending the surrounding satyrs flying through the air. Chari felt himself stand. His legs moved forward, no longer crippled by exhaustion.

A pike-holding satyr charged from the left. With a wave of Chari's hand, it was tossed into the air and slammed brutally into a wall. The sound of bones cracking echoed through the chamber. Another beast lunged from the right. Purple lightning left its body in a spasm on the ground. Using Chari's body, Zajur cut a swathe through the crowd of cowering satyrs until he reached the one with the ritual knife. It reached forward to stab Seya, but its body was abruptly stopped. Chari's hand reached out towards it, lifting it off the ground. Purple wind swirled around its body. The remaining satyrs fled, squealing and snorting in terror.

With a push of Chari's hand, the floating satyr flew forward, slamming into the altar, smashing through it, shattering the black stone, bouncing off the monolith and leaving it cracked. Its lifeless body came to a rest on the ground.

"You fool!" the Mad God screamed, before vanishing with the wind and dust.

Chari collapsed next to Seya. She shook her head, as if she were coming out of a dream, then noticing Chari lying next to her, started shaking him.

"Chari! Wake up, Chari!"

"It's okay..." he managed to say. "I'm okay."

Chari put a hand to his side. His shirt was still wet, but the pike wound was gone.

"Get up, Chari. I want to go home..."

Chari did not let go of her hand until they were standing on the grass far outside the cave. It was the greenest grass he had ever seen.

"*What wonderful colors!*" Zajur exclaimed.

"*What happens now?*" Chari asked the demon.

"*I am free now.*"

"*Is it over? What about the Mad God?*"

"*My chains to my master have been cut forever. With his shrine broken, the Mad God no longer has the power to influence this world. I can go wherever I like...for now. That's a nice sunset, maybe I'll just drift right into it.*"

"*You're not going to do any demon stuff to people, are you?*"

"Who me? Certainly not. I've never cared for that line of work, never had the heart to hurt people. Well, people who didn't have it coming. That's why I needed to get away. Away from the Mad God, away from the taskmasters, and the demons, away from the nether realm."

"Maybe you could help people?"

"Maybe. But that is none of your concern. Our bargain is complete."

"None of my—"

But the spirit was gone.

"Zajur?" Chari said aloud.

"Is he gone?" Seya asked.

"I think so."

Seya smiled up at him. "My voice is gone, too."

The statement shook Chari's mind to momentary blankness. Then a new idea came to him. Was it possible? Was the girl freed from her madness? Was the Mad God truly banished? His thoughts drifted to what Zajur had said. *For now.*

There could be a whole lot of *now* in now.

"Let's go home, brother," she said, tugging at his arm.

He returned the smile, feeling an immeasurable weight lift from his soul. "Okay. Let's go home."

Chari took Seya's tiny hand and led her down the hill, across the river and the trade road, through the woods, to the back of a quiet little village where the evening meals were just being served.

THE END

ABOUT THE AUTHORS

James Barnes

Biography

Originally from the Oregon Coast, James W. Barnes is a freelance writer who acquired a Masters in Theology in 1986. He began teaching that same year, eventually accepting a job in New Zealand, where he currently resides. He is the author of "Sea Songs: Readers Theatre from the South Pacific" and James has also published short works in *Takahe* and *North and South*, both New Zealand-based magazines. He is currently working on a new fantasy novel "A Page in Time".

Social Media Links

Website: https://npcopywriter.wordpress.com/
Facebook: https://www.facebook.com/jim.barnes.31
Instagram: https://www.instagram.com/shrydlander/

Nikola Chalakov

Biography

Nikola Chalakov is the author of novels such as *The Iron Scepter* and *Rozara's Trial*, as well as *The Circle of Moonlight*; a collection of short stories set in the same world as *Rozara's Trial*. Born in Bulgaria, Nikola is a writer and translator in French and English, and he has translated the Bulgarian Academy of Sciences: World Heritage of Bulgaria, Bulgarian Calendar Holidays and Observances, and 150 years Bulgarian Academy of Sciences. Nikola devotes to learning new things and improving his craft, he loves to immerse himself into new worlds of any book genre.

Social Media Links

Website: https://nikolachalakov.com/
Instagram:
https://www.instagram.com/nikola_chalakov/ Twitter:
https://twitter.com/nikola_bathory

Shawn Cowling

Biography

Shawn Cowling has been writing stories for over a decade, starting with a serial fiction piece at *Jukepop Serials*. He spends most of his time over at his blog, where you can find a treasure trove of flash fiction, a podcast: *We Have a Situation Here*; where a new short story comes to life in under 40 minutes every week, board games, and other fun stuff. When not writing fiction, he spends his days doing process and statistical analysis wishing for a solid good versus evil story to show up in a scatter plot. To date, this has not happened. You can also find several books by Shawn on Amazon, such as *People on the Highway* (now available in yellow and green!).

Social Media Links
Website: https://shawncowling.wordpress.com/

Ryan Cutler

Biography

Ryan Cutler has spent his life on the coast of South England. Having completed a degree in Media and Communications, he now works as a copywriter and writes fantasy fiction on the side. "The Twilight Guide" is his first published story, inspired by tabletop roleplaying adventures and his years of exploring the English countryside. He is also in the process of writing long-form fantasy literature inspired by Celtic mythology for eventual publication. His other hobbies include reading, gaming, tabletop RPGs, and historical research.

Social Media Links
Website: https://rscutlercreative.wordpress.com

Some Favorite Things
Books: Witcher, LOTR, Kings of the Wyld, Star Wars
Genres: High Fantasy, Sci-Fi, Historical Fiction, Celtic Fantasy

Elana Gomel

Biography

Elana Gomel was born in a country that no longer exists, and since then has lived in several others. She currently resides in California. She is an academic with a long list of books and articles, specializing in science fiction, Victorian literature, and serial killers. She is also a fiction writer and the author of more than a hundred short stories, several novellas, and four novels. Her story "Where the Streets Have No Name" was the winner of the 2020 Gravity Award, and her story "Mine Seven" is included in The Best Horror of the Year 13 edited by Ellen Datlow. Her latest fiction publications are Little Sister and Black House, a fantasy novel. She is a member of HWA.

Social Media Links

Website: https://www.citiesoflightanddarkness.com/
Facebook: https://www.facebook.com/elana.gomel
Twitter: https://twitter.com/ElanaGomel
Instagram: https://www.instagram.com/elanagomel/

K.A. Kenny

Biography

K.A. Kenny marches to the sound of the guns, often on a whim, and where others would not imagine going. He has an MA in History from George Washington University. After a career in technical analysis, K. A. turned his talents to the serious business of speculative fiction. Last year, in addition to "The Tale of Lady Evangeline" in OMAM, his story "Never Leave Me" was published in Altered Reality, and "The Avian Project" was published in Across the Margin. He sold his SF novel The Starflower to Austin Macauley last December, and it is due to be published in late 2022. He is currently working on a horror story "The Looalee". K. A. lives with his wife Carole and dogs Freya and Cato in Virginia's Blue Ridge Mountains.

Social Media Links

Website: https://keithkennyblog.wordpress.com/

DonnaRae Menard

Biography

DonnaRae Menard carried her love for writing throughout her life, even bringing it into her workplace where she would write scenes from the office and secretly leave them around. She is the author of *Murder in The Meadow*, *Willa the Wisp*, and a self-published historical fiction *In the Shadow of Pharaoh*. She has also written short stories in *The Clarion Anthology*, *The Bould Awards Anthology*. Her latest work *Murder on Eagle Drop Ridge* will continue to follow Katelyn Took from her previous book *Murder in The Meadow*. She writes for the love of the word and invites anyone to sit for a cup of coffee and chat it up. Her current project is *The Waif and the Warlord* with OMAM.

Social Media Links

Website: https://www.donnaraemenardbooks.com/

Richard Reydan

Biography
Richard Reydan heralds from England and is of Irish gypsy and Yorkshire stock. He has degrees in psychology and social science. Richard spent his youth traveling the world, learning a yarn or two from many indigenous communities. Now settled down, he writes alongside his faithful companion, a small terrier he rescued while on his global travels. An experienced plot writer for Live Action Role Play, Richard has written fantasy stories since he could hold a pen. His favorite authors include Bernard Cornwall, Ken Follett, Joe Abercrombie, Anthony Ryan. His current work in progress is an epic fantasy set within a Celtic background.

Social Media Links
Facebook: www.facebook.com/RichardReydanWriter

Ben Sherman

Biography

Ben Sherman is the author of various fantasy and science fiction literature, with a penchant for grimdark fantasy. His introduction into writing was when he became an ardent reader in middle school, opening up R.A. Salvatore's "The Thousand Orcs," and Tolkien's "The Hobbit." He has been writing and world building for twelve years as of 2022, and when he's not writing he's either reading, gaming, or spending time with his dogs. Ben has a long fascination with martial arts, both eastern and western, and he majored in history at Samford University.

Some Favorite Things

Books: The Drizzt Series, The Gotrek & Felix Series, The Stand, Blades of The Moonsea, The Blacktongue

Films: The Lord of The Rings Trilogy, Kingdom of Heaven, The Last Samurai, Sword of The Stranger, any Clint Eastwood Western

Douglas W.T. Smith

Biography
Douglas W.T. Smith is the author of *Shadow of the Wicked*, which ranked in Amazon Top 5 List in Dark Fantasy and Sword and Sorcery eBooks in 2021. Hailing from Australia, the driest of any continent on earth other than Antarctica, his debut full length novel *To Wield the Stars* is due out with OMAM in 2022. Between writing and reading fantasy stories, Douglas embarks on adventures in nature with his wife, son, and beloved dog. If you want to know when Douglas' next book will come out, please visit his website, where you can sign up to receive news about his upcoming projects.

Social Media Links
Website: www.dwtsmith.com
Facebook: https://www.facebook.com/authordouglaswtsmith
Instagram:
https://www.instagram.com/douglas.w.t.smith
TikTok: https://www.tiktok.com/@douglaswtsmithh

Olyn Warfield

Biography

Olyn Warfield is a poet and the author of a three-book saga, monthly serials, and contributor to several anthologies. She strives to produce entertainment that exceeds the reader's expectations and enjoyment of anthropomorphic (furry) adventures. Her blog, "My Dog Leads Two Lives," shares the adventures of her beloved Omar Blue, where he can thrive in a fantasy after-life existence as the pack leader in a mysterious wilderness, where all canines are welcome. When Olyn isn't writing she can be found tending to her garden and taking long walks with her dog, Babee Blue, while enjoying open skies, landscapes, and fresh air.

Social Media Links
Website: https://omarblue.blogspot.com/
Facebook: https://www.facebook.com/Omarblue2/

JM Williams

Biography

JM Williams is the author of *In the Valley of Magic*, *Call of the Guardian*, and other works of fantasy and science fiction. He has published around fifty short fiction pieces in a range of venues including *Over My Dead Body! Mystery Magazine*, *The Arcanist*, and The *New Accelerator*, and is a co-founder Of Metal and Magic Publishing. JM currently serves as Editor-in-Chief, working with an international team of writers. He lives in Korea with his wife and cats. He spends most of his time these days editing new OMAM content.

Social Media Links

Website: http://jmwilliams.home.blog
Facebook: http://facebook.com/jmwwriting

Benjamin Zahm

Biography
Benjamin Zahm lives in the land of ten thousand lakes, otherwise known as Minnesota. Benjamin's love for fantasy began at a young age and was greatly influenced by JRR Tolkien's *The Lord of the Rings*, Brian Jacques *Redwall* series, and several interactive novels from *Delight Games*. These were among the many works which inspired him to pursue creative writing whenever he gets the chance. When Benjamin is not happily reading (or writing) fantasy adventures, he enjoys getting together with family and friends to play various sports and be outdoors.

Some Favorite Things
Activities: Hockey, snowboarding, ultimate frisbee, spikeball, and disc golf
Books: Redwall Series, The Lord of the Rings

ABOUT THE EDITOR

Allison Filiatreault is a staff editor at *Of Metal and Magic Publishing* and hails from the southern part of Quebec. Growing up, she loved to be outdoors, hiking or going to her favorite zoo/animal rehab; where they nursed the local wildlife back to health. She can still be found outside on a hiking trail or in her garden, where she has turned it into a pollinator's paradise. Her love for writing fantasy began at a young age, when her Grade 2 teacher made the class write a short story. She would continue to write for herself, developing worlds in the fantasy realms and eventually a sci-fi world. Her first step into editing happened in university, when she was asked by fellow students to take a look over their work and help improve it. She has recently combined her love of writing with her passions for the environment and biodiversity.

Greetings from
Of Metal and Magic

If you've come this far, you must have enjoyed what you read! At OMAM, we strive to publish the most thrilling, adventurous, and exciting stories. If you liked this book, you can do us a big favor by leaving a review on your preferred platform.

Of Metal and Magic Publishing was founded in 2020 by veteran authors Richie Billing and JM Williams, with a focus on quality epic and high fantasy fiction.

The collaboration began many years prior when Richie, JM, and a handful of other authors came together to create a new fantasy world. Our international menagerie crafted stories which all took place in the same epic fantasy setting. We developed a unique method of storytelling that involves writing in the same shared fantasy universe, which we each populate with our characters, cultures and stories. Through hard work and heated debates, we developed a unified canon and history for our world, SORIA.

Though they are designed as stand-alone works, our stories all influence the greater narrative of our shared world, even directly referencing or overlapping with each other. We refer to these Soria stories, relating to our original fantasy world, as *Of Metal and Magic* CORE stories.

But we do much more than our CORE series. It is this innovative and unique format of shared worlds that *Of Metal and Magic Publishing* wishes to build on. In addition to seeking out new voices and the best talent in the traditional fantasy genre, we also seek to craft new worlds for our authors and contributors to relish and share. Every single story published by OMAM has the potential to grow into something greater, a new epic world of shared narratives.

The OMAM team has been writing and publishing for years and felt that, with all of our combined experiences, we could create a publisher which could give opportunities to new and exciting voices in the world of fantasy, help and support writers with their careers, and above all, contribute to the world of writing in new and exciting ways. To that end, you can check out our sponsored podcast, *The Fantasy Writers' Toolshed*—available on Spotify, Google Play, YouTube, and other major podcast hosts.

As a publisher, we are always looking for submissions from new authors. In addition to publishing novels in our signature flavor, we also publish short fiction on our website and in occasional anthologies. We are also not averse to fantasy verse. If you're a fantasy author, whatever your chosen format, send us your work.

To find out more about who we are and what we do, or to submit your work for potential publication, look us up at http://ofmetalandmagicpublishing.wordpress.com, or on sign up for our NEWSLETTER, for all the updates plus some free goodies.

Discover more epic fantasy at:

http://ofmetalandmagicpublishing.wordpress.com